A Stroke of Luck

R. A. Hutchins

ISBN: 9798534993134

For Andrew,
Who is named after the Scottish town in which
this story is set,
You make me proud every day!
Love you so much xxx

CONTENTS

The Albatross (Family: Diomedeidae)

Albatrosses comprise between 13 and 24 species of very large seabirds, living mainly in the Southern Ocean and the North Pacific. The name "albatross" originally comes from Arabic (meaning "the diver") and then Portuguese in the word alcatraz (meaning "gannet"). This is also the origin of the name of the famous island prison in San Francisco harbour.

Albatrosses are some of the largest flying birds. For example, the Wandering albatross (*Diomedea exulans*) can have wingspans up to 12 feet across. They are also the most efficient travellers of all the vertebrates on this planet, able to fly hundreds of miles without flapping their wings. They typically feed on fish, octopus and squid which they catch by making shallow dives from the surface of the ocean using their long, hooked bills.

Albatrosses can also be extremely long-lived. The Laysan albatross (*Phoebastria immutabilis*) lives up to 50 years on average, but one female called Wisdom was hatched in 1951 and is now believed to be the oldest confirmed wild bird in the world. She most recently hatched a chick in early 2021.

Albatrosses live in colonies on remote oceanic islands. Once hatched, young birds learn a series of elaborate breeding rituals and "dances" which include preening, pointing, calling, bill clacking, and staring. They will "dance" with many partners for several years, until they select one partner, and a Pair bond is formed. The Pair bonds last for the life of the pair.

Pairs will also invest significant time and effort in raising their chicks, potentially taking over a year from egg-laying to fledging. They will take turns incubating the egg and gathering food. This unusual behaviour (for birds) significantly improves reproductive success and is important as only one egg is laid every couple of years.

One of the most famous mentions of the Albatross was in *The Rime of the Ancient Mariner* written by the poet Samuel Taylor Coleridge (1772-1834). It tells of the story of the Mariner, an old, grey-bearded sailor, who had set sail on a long sea voyage. At the time, albatrosses were seen as a good omen and, in the poem, a single albatross leads the ship out of danger. But the Mariner shoots the albatross with a crossbow, leading to misfortune for the ship. The Mariner is then forced to wear the dead albatross around his neck as a symbol of the fatal curse he has brought on the crew.

ONE

Phoebe took long, determined strides back along the beach in the small fishing village of Pittenweem. She tried to tamp down the feelings evoked by the beautiful proposal she had just witnessed, but succeeded only to bring her focus more firmly to the facts at hand. She was alone on an extremely painful anniversary. Living closer to home than ever before in her adult life, and farther away from her dream of studying albatrosses in the North Pacific. Indeed, her days were soon to be filled with collecting, analysing and measuring seal poo – how glamorous! Not quite the Hawaiian island life she had planned when she gave up everything to follow her passion.

Wishing she had brought a coat, as despite the sun there was a cold nip in the air, Phoebe rubbed her arms absentmindedly. She ascended the battered stone staircase from the beach and made her way along the harbour to where her car was parked. She considered stopping in the coffee shop, but everyone seemed to be crowding in the window, cheering the couple on the beach, so Phoebe rushed past with her head down, deciding to find a tea shop in nearby Anstruther before returning to the small flat she was sharing with her best friend in St. Andrews.

When the decision on the grant proposal had been delayed, and her research post in Oxford ended, Phoebe had been at a loss. She had already burnt all her bridges and so was relieved, though not exactly happy, when her friend from university, Melanie, told her excitedly of a six month placement at the Gatty Marine Lab in St. Andrews. Part of the Scottish Oceans Institute, which would admittedly look good on her resume. Soon to be made homeless and jobless, Phoebe had applied, knowing she was woefully overqualified for the post. And so, just two weeks ago, she had arrived in the quaint Fife town, her old Ford overflowing with her every possession. Not needing to start work until the beginning of May, Phoebe had exhausted all the tourist delights the area had to offer. Twice. She was now beginning to dwell in her thoughts too often, the regrets and questions swirling around until she was an anxious mess. This day in particular, she could do with some company. A specific person's company, in fact, though that wasn't to be.

The drive to Anstruther took barely five minutes along the coast, and Phoebe found a parking spot easily. There was a choice of chocolate shop or old-fashioned tearoom, and Phoebe chose the latter, settling herself in a window seat and exhaling slowly. She checked her phone for messages, seeing none and not expecting any. When she had cut off from her old life she had done so resolutely and effectively. Another small pang in her chest. Another layer of regret. Phoebe pulled out her old faithful – a book from her childhood, battered and well-thumbed. It was the reason for her interest in the albatross, and detailed each different species of the bird, their habitats, breeding, diets – everything the budding scientist needed to know. Having her biology degree and PhD under her belt, plus numerous research positions in the UK, all that remained was for thirty-three year old Phoebe to actually go halfway around the world and study the birds in their natural habitat. A dream which seemed more distant now than ever before. She had given up so much, and for what?

"Here's your tea, dearie, can I get you any cake with that? A scone maybe?" The small, rotund woman had a cheerful smile and Phoebe couldn't help smiling back.

"No, thank you, this is fine."

The woman hovered, her curiosity getting the better of her.

"On holiday then?"

"No, ah, well I'm just visiting Anstruther yes, but I've recently moved to St. Andrews."

"Ah, beautiful town. Great golf!" she made her way back to the counter, pausing to chat to a table of four men who were squashed into the corner. All middle aged, they were chatting loudly in American accents about the golf memorabilia which adorned the chintzy walls. Their attire gave them away as lovers of the sport and Phoebe supressed a shudder. She had been made acutely aware since her arrival in the area that the title of 'Home of Golf' was taken very seriously in St. Andrews. Not just in the many shops which catered for tourists of the sport, but also in the numerous golf courses and instructors. Golf here was big business. It was just a shame Phoebe couldn't stand the activity. Tedious and boring, she had no intention of ever taking it up.

Looking up as the small bell above the door chimed, a younger man, equally dressed for the golf course, entered. He paused for a moment upon catching sight of Phoebe, gave her a blatantly interested look, winked and then moved on to the table of four. *Urgh*, Phoebe thought to herself, *really?*

"Are you ready for the next course, gentlemen," his accent, southern European Phoebe guessed, grated on her for no reason other than she was finding everything annoying today. She sipped her tea and focussed on her book, trying to ignore when they all squeezed past her on their way out, the newcomer making a mock bow to the woman behind the counter and saying, "Thank you, beautiful as always my darling Edna," to which the woman blushed and fussed over her apron happily.

Considering herself an independent woman, Phoebe found this kind of male attention patronising and off putting, so refused to look up as he passed her for a second time. This was why she preferred birds. Much simpler.

TWO

Mark sat on the balcony of his small, rented condo, listening to the sounds of nature which surrounded him on all sides. He was thankful he had chosen to live off campus, away from his colleagues and the Stanford student population. He had only been here for six months, a short time Mark knew, yet he had struggled to make friends and fit in. Mostly from a lack of enthusiasm on his own part. At thirty-six, Mark was having trouble starting over from scratch – not just with his job and in a new location, a new continent in fact, but also coming to terms with the fact he was now single. He certainly didn't feel footloose and fancy free! This was his dream, for all of his adult life, teaching in a top university, living in the sunshine state, surrounded by the best in his field. But why did it not feel like cloud nine?

He took the last swig from his now-warm bottle of beer and retreated back indoors to what had become his nightly routine – an hour on the exercise bike, a shower, and two hours of work on his laptop before bed. It kept the loneliness at bay. Until, that is, the insomnia took its turn, and Mark spent most of each night watching random shows or typing and then deleting emails to his ex. He was existing, rather than living, and he had no idea how to break the cycle.

THREE

Phoebe shrugged out of her coat and hung it in the hallway closet, unzipping her boots with a sigh. The romantic scene from earlier had stayed with her, making her think of her own proposal, received some three years ago. It hadn't been romantic on a grand scale, no picnic lunch and well-prepared declaration on the beach like the couple she had seen, but it had moved her nonetheless.

Ever the scientist, her partner had been caught in the lab longer than he'd intended, and Phoebe had come to look for him after finally shutting down her own computer in the next building. Their dinner reservation had long since passed and, on becoming aware of the time, he had seemed unusually ruffled. Taking her out onto the roof terrace of the building, ostensibly to take a look through the new telescope he was working on, the man had fumbled and flustered until he caught Phoebe off guard – dropping to one knee and popping the question. Of course, she'd said yes. You don't date someone for four years, move to Oxford to continue your research closer to him, and then turn him down.

Besides, Phoebe loved him. Had loved him, she corrected herself mentally. That was all in the past now and she needed to move on. Checking the flat for Melanie and finding it empty, Phoebe sat at the kitchen table, opened her laptop and checked for emails in case he'd finally decided to contact her. Finding none, and not having honestly expected something anyway, given that she was the one who had chosen her career over him, Phoebe rested her head in her hands. She was weary with trying to fill her empty days. Weary of attempting to distract her head and her heart. Used to working long hours in the lab, she couldn't wait for her new post to start properly. The sooner the better, in fact.

In the past, when she felt like this, Phoebe would have prayed – for a sense of peace, for confirmation of purpose, to give thanks for what she had been given in life. For nearly a year now, those prayers had slowly dried up, leaving Phoebe feeling as if she were at sea without an anchor, constantly moving, always adrift.

"Hi-de-hi!" the chirpy sound of Melanie's greeting brought Phoebe back from her glum inner voice.

"Hello!" she forced a happy tone and stood up to welcome her friend back, "Good day?"

"Same old, same old, it'll be much better next week when you're there with me!" Melanie squeezed her tight in an affectionate hug and Phoebe returned it as best she could, generally uncomfortable with shows of emotion. "Shall we go out tonight? See if there's any talented golfers that take our fancy?" Melanie winked and giggled, an expression which served only to remind Phoebe of the sleazy man from earlier in the tearoom.

"I'm quite tired actually," she saw her friend's face fall, and yet Phoebe couldn't seem to bring herself to change her mind.

"Oh, well, do you mind if I go? Some of the people from the lab are meeting up at the Nineteenth Watering Hole on South Street later on."

"Of course, I've got… preparation and unpacking to do anyway," Phoebe fibbed, standing to begin making their evening meal while Melanie went upstairs for a shower. Despite being the same age as Phoebe, and actually quite shy, Mel was still very much living the single life, and showed no signs of settling down. Phoebe knew she should force herself to go out, to start making new friends and integrating into her new community. But not tonight. Tonight, as with every night since she'd arrived, Phoebe couldn't face the prospect of answering questions about herself and her past. It was better to hide away here. Alone.

Carlos cast a quick glance around the bar as he entered, partly to make sure there were none of today's clients – he had used up his daily quota of patience for small-talk both on and off the course already – and partly to scout out any desirable females who might be appreciative of his attentions. The large group in the corner caught his eye. Mainly men, there were only three women, of which one looked up as he entered. She was fair skinned and had straight, blonde hair which fell in a bob around her petite face. Carlos ordered his usual and wondered how he could extract the beauty from the group long enough to talk to her.

Lady Luck was on his side, as shortly after he took a stool at the end of the bar, she got up to visit the bathroom. Carlos waited impatiently until he saw the woman round the corner on her return, before jumping from his perch, landing as gracefully as a cat who has spotted a mouse.

"Good evening," his said, blocking the woman's path back to her table. Far from the haughty response he was getting used to, which was so far removed from the flirty women back home in Portugal, this lady actually smiled and giggled, her blue eyes sparkling brightly. *Was she drunk or just starved of attention?* he wondered.

"Hello!"

"What is a nice Senhora like you doing in a place like this?" It was lame, he knew, but she had actually caught him off guard by not rebuffing his advances at the first hurdle.

More giggles.

"I'm with my work colleagues actually. Melanie, that's my name," she extended her hand to him shyly.

"Carlos, very pleased to make the acquaintance of such a beauty!"

She blushed deeply and Carlos knew his compliment had hit the mark. He was unsure where to go from here. He was actually quite shy under all the façade, and used to the flirty banter in his home tongue, which flowed smoothly and was met with equal gusto. Here, things were different. Everything was taken so much more … seriously. The woman opposite, who looked about thirty, smiled up at him expectantly. Carlos cleared his throat.

"Can I get you a drink?" he asked, hopefully.

"Ah, I'd better be getting back to my table," Melanie looked genuinely sad at the fact, "Perhaps another night?" The hope in her eyes was clear to see, and Carlos jumped at the chance to arrange a date with her.

"Excellent, tomorrow perhaps? At the little Italian restaurant by the harbour?"

"A meal? Oh, well, yes, that sounds lovely," Melanie stumbled over her words, wringing her hands nervously.

"Perfect Senhora, I will meet you there at eight?"

"Yes, yes thank you," Melanie scooted past him and returned to her seat, her face blushing a deep red.

Carlos resumed his perch at the bar. He hadn't for a second expected that glib chat up line to work. He needed to polish up his act. And fast.

FOUR

Mark smiled at the department secretary, Crystal, as she stood up from the large table in the conference room, her minute-taking notebook tucked under her arm neatly. The others had left the room quickly after the meeting, whilst Mark had been distracted finishing his notes on his laptop.

"So, honey, you settling in okay?" she asked kindly.

"Well, it's been six months..." Mark tried to avoid the question, packing his laptop bag quickly under her thoughtful scrutiny. She had the air of a very wise woman, despite being still only in her twenties.

"Yes... but you aren't very settled yet are you?" the question cut straight to the heart of the matter, and Mark couldn't help but nod.

"I, well, no I guess not," he shrugged his shoulders, feeling the hollowness in the pit of his stomach which had been ever-present since Mark had boarded the plane at Heathrow six months before.

"And you're sure, this was the right move, honey?" For having no idea as to his past, nor what he'd left behind, this woman was certainly hitting the bullseye.

Mark decided to be honest, for the first time, with her and with himself, "No, I'm not certain. I, ah, I'm hoping I'll turn the corner soon, and it'll all click into place."

"Mhm," she didn't sound convinced, and Mark scurried from the room, feeling like a child leaving the Principal's office.

FIVE

One more day, Phoebe told herself the next morning, *one more day to fill, then the weekend with Melanie, then work on Monday. You can do this.* Melanie had long since left for the lab, having rolled in after midnight the night before. Phoebe had not spoken to her since the previous evening. She couldn't bear to sit around all day though, so pulling on her boots and coat, Phoebe headed out onto North Street, turning right in the direction of the Old Course. It was not the hotel complex and golf courses which drew her, though, rather it was the magnificent beach which ran alongside. Named West Sands, the beach stretched for two glorious miles, famous for being the location used in the opening scenes of the film 'Chariots of Fire'. Today was overcast and chilly, so Phoebe hoped the beach would be quite deserted. She was annoyed at herself, that she had come to such a beautiful part of the world and yet was having to force herself to enjoy it.

Drawn, as always, to its solitary silence, with no sound but the rustling of the wind through the dunes and the waves crashing onto the shore, Phoebe found herself sitting on the sand. She enjoyed feeling the silkiness of it as she took handfuls and watched as it slid through her fingers. She was alone, bar a solitary dog walker who took the path closest to the waves, letting his black Labrador frolic in the water. The man was tall, even at this distance, and he caught Phoebe's eye for a moment, making her think of another tall man she once knew.

Trying hard not to let her mind wander again, Phoebe took her favourite book from her backpack once more, settled her reading glasses on her nose and flicked to the chapter on longevity. The life span of the albatross always impressed Phoebe, with some of the birds living over fifty years with the same life partner. This thought brought the emotion to Phoebe's throat and she struggled to clear it. *I will not cry!* she chided herself, turning instead to a page about wing span.

"Into golf, then?" The voice came from behind, over

Phoebe's shoulder, making her jump.

"Excuse me?" She spun on the spot, glaring at the stranger.

"Albatross, it says, like in golf!" He spoke slowly as if she were clearly stupid to have not got his reference in the first place. His heavy accent and beautifully tanned skin spoke of an origin which was not Scottish. Phoebe shielded her eyes against the weak glare of the spring sun which had finally made an appearance, to get a better look at the man, realising with a sinking feeling that he was the winker from the teashop yesterday.

"No, it's albatross as in actual albatross. The bird!" Phoebe added, the tone of exasperation evident in her voice. She turned back to her book, dismissing the stranger silently.

Not to be perturbed, however, he sat down next to her, graceful as a swan. Phoebe let out an audible sigh of irritation, hoping to make it quite clear she did not intend to converse further.

"So, you are not a golfer?" He asked, his eyebrow quirked in question, his mouth a half smile.

"Indeed, I am not," Phoebe assumed her haughtiest tone, "I am a scientist!"

"Really? That sounds very… interesting," he searched for a word, though mocked her with his expression. Clearly it was not an interesting enough subject to pursue, as he returned to his original subject, "An albatross is a golfing term, you know!"

"Really?" Phoebe could not have sounded more bored.

"Yes, it means three under par. Par is…"

"I really have no interest," Phoebe cut him off short.

"I see," his large brown eyes morphed into a puppy dog look. He was obviously used to making women weak at the knees with this one, but it had no effect on Phoebe. She was sworn off men, the indent of her wedding ring still visible on her naked finger. Besides, he was not at all her type, giving off the air of a ladies' man if ever there was one.

The heavy silence thrummed between them uncomfortably, until he himself sighed, "I did not catch your name, Senhora?"

"I did not give it."

"I am Carlos Ferreira, Pleased to meet you." He held out his hand, which Phoebe had absolutely no intention of taking. She pinned her loose curls behind her ear and focused resolutely on the waves ahead.

21

"A pleasure," he muttered taking his hand back and standing, brushing the sand from his behind and onto Phoebe as he did so. Carlos strode off through the dunes, and Phoebe did not turn to watch him leave. An uncomfortable intrusion which she could have done without. Her nerves, already frayed, were now totally shredded, so Phoebe stood up reluctantly and turned into the wind, checking that her precious book was safely stored away in her bag before heading along the beach towards the main road and then in the direction of the castle ruins.

SIX

Another day of research interspersed with teaching complete, Marc wondered morosely if he should join his colleagues for a Friday night beer. He was sweating and had forgotten to bring a new, clean shirt to keep in his office, the previous having already been used. An oversight he had berated himself for repeatedly. Mark was saved from having to make the decision, however, when he received a call from his mother, sounding frantic.

"Mark, Mark is that you?"

Who else would it be? he wondered, before replying as clearly as he could,

"Yes, Mum, it's Mark. We spoke on Sunday, it's only Friday, is something wrong?" Mark preferred to keep routines in his life, and his Sunday evening call with his parents was one of them. They were getting on a bit now, and being an only child he worried about them. He also liked to come straight to the point, unnecessary waffle annoyed him.

"Yes," she began crying then, and Mark sat down on the nearest bench, the ebb and flow of campus moving around him unseen. It had been years, decades even, since he'd seen his mother cry and his heartrate immediately increased with concern.

"Hey, Mum, take a deep breath. What's happened?"

"It's your father, he's… he's… " *Oh God, please don't let him be dead. I need to see him, speak to him, explain what happened with…*

"He's what, Mum?" Mark tried to keep the worry and impatience from his voice.

"In the hospital!" she finally whispered and Mark let out the breath he had been unconsciously holding.

"Why?" he asked, not sure if he wanted the answer. His dad had suffered from heart disease for the past nine years.

"Heart attack. It's bad this time, son," she sniffed and hiccoughed on the other end of the line and Mark swallowed down the lump in his own throat.

"I'm on my way, Mum, I'm on my way… tell him to hang in there!"

SEVEN

"Yes, tonight!" Melanie had the impression that Phoebe was not paying attention, as she described the date which she was looking forward to with Carlos that evening. The bed was strewn with discarded outfit choices, and Melanie was sweating from the stress and effort of it all. "It would help if I had a little input!" she let her exasperation show, and finally Phoebe looked up from her perch on the swivel desk chair in the corner of the bedroom.

"Sorry, Mel, in my own little world at the mo!"

"I'd noticed!" Melanie took a deep breath in and went over to her friend, "Call him, Mel, call him and put yourself out of this misery!"

"I can't. It's over!" Phoebe's voice quivered and she struggled to hold in the tears which threatened to spill out. "Anyway, tell me again about this mystery guy… you literally just met him last night?"

"Yes, and he's good looking and charming, but I'm feeling the nerves now. Fancy joining us like we did at uni? A bit of moral support?"

"Really, I'm not feeling…"

"Oh, come on, Phoebe! If you won't call him, then you need to snap out of it!" Melanie regretted her harsh tone, but her words held truth.

Phoebe knew her friend was right, and felt bad that she had been shutting her out since she'd arrived. It was Mel, after all, who had invited her to share her flat, Mel who had told her about the job opportunity.

"Okay, I'll come for a drink, then leave you two to eat together," she compromised reluctantly.

"Perfect! Now, black or green dress?"

'On The Grapevine' had only been open for a few months, nestled down at the bottom of North Street, past the cathedral ruins and down the hill near to the harbour. It was popular with the large student population of the town, and with the tourists. The locals preferred the more traditional eateries. Tottering down the bank in her high-heeled, strappy sandals, Melanie clung to Phoebe's arm.

"Look, there he is!" she announced in a stage whisper, though Carlos was nowhere near being in earshot.

Phoebe followed the direction of her friend's eyes, "It can't be!" she muttered to herself.

"Can't be what?"

"Um, I think I recognise the guy," Phoebe was stopped from commenting further by their arrival at the restaurant. Carlos gave a wide-eyed look at the two women opposite him, before hiding his surprise behind the usual mask of chivalry.

"Well, good evening, beautiful ladies! Am I to be graced with the presence of both of you?"

"Just for a drink," Phoebe replied quickly, "then the lucky Mel has you all to herself," the sarcastic tone was not lost on any of them, and Melanie gave Phoebe a sharp dig in the ribs as they followed Carlos into the weathered, brick building. They found a table in the seating area which was separate from the main restaurant and Carlos took their drinks order to the bar.

"What is it now?" Mel whispered, "Why so rude?"

"I've met him before. Not properly… just, I think he might be a bit sleazy!"

"Sleazy? He seemed charming to me!"

"Well, you've never been the best judge of men…" Phoebe regretted the words as soon as they were out of her mouth. She saw Melanie huff and turn her attention to Carlos, giving him a huge smile and earning them a wink in return. When he finally made his way back to the table, balancing the drinks on a tray on one hand like a pro, the air between the two women was positively icy.

"So, ah, you have had the good day?" Carlos directed the question at Mel, who was making a point of looking at him as if he were the only other person in the place.

"Yes, very good, thank you. Work, but of course I had tonight to look forward to!" she gave a girlish giggle and Phoebe sighed inwardly. She would like to have thought this display was for her benefit, but she knew that Mel was an outrageous flirt, especially once she had the first glass of wine inside to bolster her courage. Sitting like a third wheel, Phoebe retreated into her own thoughts once more, her mind always flitting back to him, her husband. *Ex-husband,* she corrected herself. His deep brown eyes, his Scottish lilt… Phoebe shook her head to clear the intrusive thoughts.

"And you? I am sorry, I still do not have the name?" Phoebe realised with a start that Carlos was directing the question to her.

"Phoebe, ah, Phoebe Ross. Thank you for the drink," her voice sounded stilted and awkward, rude almost, and Phoebe cringed inwardly. Clearly, she was not ready to return to the social scene. Downing her remaining wine in one huge gulp, she nodded at Carlos, gave an apologetic look to Melanie, and stood up abruptly. "Anyway, have a great evening!"

Way to embarrass yourself, Phoebs! she chastised herself as she left the restaurant, deciding to walk through the cathedral ruins to clear her head. Even at this late hour, there were a few tourists with cameras, posing for pictures, and a few locals walking their dogs. Phoebe sat on a patch of grass, in the middle of what would have been the main chapel, and drew her knees up to her chin morosely. The grant application which she had hoped to hear back about several months ago was still outstanding, so her hopes were not completely dashed yet, but why did she no longer feel hopeful about it?

Everything. She had given up everything to make her research dream a reality, so why did it feel like she had come back to square one? Single, in temporary employment, starting afresh. Phoebe sighed, quickly pulling her hand from where she had been leaning on it on the grass as something wet touched her fingers.

"What the..?"

"Oscar! Osc! I am so sorry!" Phoebe looked up into the kind eyes of a tall man, holding the collar of an evidently excitable Labrador, reminding her of the pair she had seen on the beach the other day.

"No problem!" Phoebe replied, smiling up at him.

They paused as if time was frozen, each staring at the other.

EIGHT

Mark felt sick. Having jumped the first available flight to Heathrow, he was now deciding whether to fly to Edinburgh and hire a car to take him to his parents' home town of Perth, or whether to hire a car now and just drive the whole distance. Given that his whole body shook from lack of sleep and too much caffeine, he decided the flight was the best option.

Once checked in, he had three hours to wait. Another three hours to wonder how severe the heart attack was, whether he would even get back in time before… before… no, he wouldn't go there. At least his parents lived nowhere near Oxford, that was a blessing as it meant there was no way he would see her. She may live rent free in his mind, but he had no desire to see his ex face to face and rake up past love and recent hurts. Images of her flashed through his mind as if on a movie reel. Smiling. Laughing. Crying. Mark shook his head to clear it and headed in the direction of the bar, deciding he definitely needed something stronger than coffee if he was to complete this last leg of the journey with his sanity intact.

NINE

The seconds added up until Phoebe became embarrassed, sitting as she was on the grass, looking up into the eyes of a stranger. She rose unsteadily to her feet, still smiling awkwardly. The dog, who was barely restrained in his excitement, lunged forwards and licked her as she stood, catching her full on the mouth.

"Oh, Oscar!" The mortification in the man's voice was clear, "I am so sorry, he's a menace, a friendly menace, but a menace none the less. He's only nine months you, see. Ah, sorry," he blushed bright red, highlighting the smattering of freckles over his cheekbones.

"Not to worry," Phoebe said, trying to discreetly wipe her mouth on her sleeve, "he's gorgeous," it was she who turned red now, looking away to hide the embarrassment that the guy might think she were referring to him. He was gorgeous, though, with his short brown hair, greying at the temples, his small, goatee beard and wide smile. Phoebe just didn't want him to know she thought so! It was so unlike her to have such an immediate positive reaction to someone. In fact, the only other person she could remember feeling like this about was her ex.

"Jack Fraser, pleased to meet you. And this is Oscar, he's clearly VERY pleased to meet you!"

Phoebe laughed gently, "Phoebe Ross, it's lovely to meet you both."

"I don't normally, I mean, I'm not in the habit of asking strangers out, but I was wondering if you'd like to get a drink with me? At a pub or a coffee shop? I know it's late, but, I, ah, sorry…" Oscar shot off to chase a pair of crows, dragging Jack with him as he still held onto the lead. Phoebe giggled as Jack struggled to rein in the feisty pup.

"Yes," she replied when he once again stood beside her, "yes, one drink would be nice."

They settled into a small table at the back of O'Reilly's pub. The Irish setting was already full, so they were lucky to get a seat as another couple left just at the right moment. Jack asked politely for Phoebe's preference, before going to the bar with their order, leaving her with the adoring Oscar. Reluctant to stay on the floor, as this did not provide nearly as much physical contact as he wanted with his new friend, the dog tried several times to jump up onto Phoebe's lap. The restrictions of the table and lack of space proved too much, however, and in the end he settled for laying his front legs – indeed the whole front half of his body – across Phoebe's knees. She giggled and rubbed him behind the ears absentmindedly, trying not to stare at the back of the stranger she had just met and who was now her drinking partner. Too late, he turned with the glasses in hand and caught Phoebe looking at him. She smiled, blushed, and swiftly returned her attention back to her canine companion.

Jack's face was a wide grin as he approached, until he saw that Phoebe was swamped by black fur and a pink nose, "Oscar, down boy! I'm so sorry, Phoebe, we haven't quite mastered the whole personal space thing yet!"

"It's fine, really, he's keeping me warm!" Phoebe laughed as the dog stubbornly refused to budge despite Jack's best efforts.

They sipped their drinks, his a pint of Guinness and hers a red wine, chatting easily. Phoebe was surprised to find herself sharing details of her life in Oxford, and at previous research posts in Inverness and Newcastle. She deliberately omitted the reasons for her move to St. Andrews, and Jack did not pry. He spoke freely of his work as a private piano tutor and part-time music teacher at the local high school, regaling Phoebe with tales of students and musical productions gone awry. Before either of them realised, it was after eleven. Phoebe could not remember the last time she had enjoyed an evening so much, or when the time had flown so quickly.

"I'm sorry to have kept you so late," Jack said, looking at his watch despondently. Phoebe hoped that he, too, wished they didn't have to part quite so quickly. "Please, let Oscar and I walk you home," the dog, who had finally settled with his whole body laying across Phoebe's feet, jumped to all fours at the sound of his name and licked his owner's hand expectantly.

"That would be lovely, thank you!" As confident and independent as she was, Phoebe didn't relish the thought of walking home alone in a new town, when she wasn't yet familiar with the old, cobbled streets and cut-throughs. "I live on North Street, down at the bottom end, I hope that's not out of your way?"

"Not at all, we actually live on Murray Park, so just around the corner!"

Phoebe breathed a sigh of relief that she was not inconveniencing the kind man, "Thank you so much!"

They threaded their way from South Street, across to Market Street and then through again onto North Street. There was a chill in the air now, and a persistent side wind, which led Phoebe to shiver as they walked. Without saying a word, Jack paused, handed her the lead, and shrugged out of his fleece jacket, dropping it around Phoebe's shoulders and being careful not to touch her as he did so. Phoebe was so touched by the thoughtful gesture, and just as much by the fact that Jack hadn't used it as an excuse to make a move on her physically, that for a moment she just stood looking at him silently.

Their eyes met in an intense gaze and neither pulled away. The same magnetism that had connected them at the cathedral ruins was back in full force and both felt it strongly.

"I, ah, shall I take the leash back?" Jack eventually broke the moment, swallowing and coughing to bring himself back to normality.

"Yes, ah, thanks," Phoebe handed a reluctant Oscar back over, and tried hard not to notice the smell of the coat which enveloped her. Fresh and woodsy, it was a pleasant assault on her senses.

When they reached her doorway, they paused. Oscar was too tired to jump up now, and lay down beside them, as Phoebe felt a strange desire to not let this man go. His presence was soothing and refreshing. A balm to her wounded soul. But she had never had a one-night stand in her life, and didn't intend to start now. The fact that Jack was clearly a gentleman, and she'd only ever slept with her husband, also factored into Phoebe's thinking, as thoughts flashed like lightening through her mind.

"So, perhaps, er, we could catch up again? Soon, I mean?" Jack's hesitancy touched Phoebe even more, and she struggled to form a coherent reply.

"Of course, I would like that! Tomorrow? I mean if you're not busy?" she realised with sudden regret how desperate that sounded and was about to backtrack.

"Yes! Yes, that would be great, shall I call round for you at four? I have classes till then."

"That's perfect!" Phoebe's heart beat fast in her chest and she felt a swell of happiness that was almost foreign to her. Worry and sadness had been her constant companions for over a year now. As she stood there, apparently rooted to the spot, Jack raised a hand in goodbye as he turned and walked away with Oscar trotting at his side. Phoebe watched his retreating form for a few seconds before rushing up the path and unlocking the front door. Too late, she realised she was still wearing his top.

TEN

Phoebe was sitting at the kitchen table just before lunchtime the next day, googling local piano tutors when Mel appeared, dishevelled and hungover from her own room. It wasn't that Phoebe didn't trust Jack, quite the opposite in fact, she was simply looking for photos of him on the internet. She took one look at her friend and stood up to put the kettle on.

"Fun night?" she asked as Mel sank into a chair, her head in her hands.

"Yes, but whisper please, my head is sore!" Mel croaked.

Phoebe smiled. Mel had never been one to hold her drink well, "I'll get you a strong coffee! How was the charming Carlos?" The sarcasm in her voice was not lost on Mel, even in her delicate state.

"Well, after the rude way you treated him, I'm surprised you're interested! But actually, the more we talked, the shyer he became. It's like, once you get behind the bravado and the façade, he's actually quite anxious and sensitive. He didn't even try to hold my hand or kiss me!" Mel sounded quite put out at the fact.

"Will you see him again?"

"Definitely! He has golf clients here for a weekend of intense coaching, but I think on Monday evening we'll meet up again," Mel had her head fully on the table now, lying sideways with her cheek against the cool wood.

"Okay, m'lady, let's get you back to bed with coffee and toast and then see if you can sleep this off!" Phoebe helped Mel up by the elbow. This wasn't the first time she'd looked after her in this state, and Phoebe doubted it would be the last. She couldn't imagine the flighty Mel settling down any time soon, despite them both nearing their mid-thirties.

Her age was a sobering thought, and Phoebe dwelt on it once she had her friend settled. She had once hoped that by now she'd be married with children of her own.

She had managed the married part, just hadn't been able to make the family part stick. Pain coursed through her heart, and Phoebe tamped it down as she always did. She had dealt with her grief by focusing on her other passion – work. Phoebe was ambitious and refused to give up on either her career or her dreams, which were heavily interlinked. When her husband had been offered a post abroad, with a salary increase and everything he'd hoped for, Mel had stubbornly and steadfastly refused to agree to the move. Instead, she had applied for her own research grant to pursue her goal of studying a species of albatross on a Hawaiian island in the North Pacific. To follow both their paths was untenable and impossible, she had argued, so Phoebe had suggested they separate, so sure was she that this was her moment to achieve her dream and that following him would simply hold her back.

Well, the research money hadn't come through – it wasn't declined, but was stuck somewhere in the process and no amount of chivvying or phone calls had resulted in an answer. Time had run out for Phoebe when her post in Oxford ended and had no funding to be renewed. Her husband had already left to begin his new life, with a broken heart to keep him company. Phoebe had swallowed any guilt and regret and ended up here. A small town in southeast Scotland, studying seal populations.

Since Phoebe's parents only lived eighty miles away near Glasgow, it felt decidedly like coming home with her tail between her legs. Not that she'd told them yet. She couldn't bear to hear their disappointment that her marriage had ended, and that she seemed to be going backwards in her career. Instead, Phoebe conducted the fortnightly calls on her mobile with deliberate care so as to not reveal any details of her recent decisions. They had never been particularly close anyway, and the last time Phoebe had seen them was her wedding some two years ago. So, she didn't feel guilty. Well, not too guilty. *What was another layer of guilt anyway?* she thought morosely as she made a cheese sandwich and sat down next to her laptop again.

As if conjured by her thoughts, Phoebe's mobile began to ring. It was not her mother though, instead it was her mother-in-law's number which appeared on the screen. Phoebe clamped both her hands together in her lap to avoid answering the call. She had been very close to Ida, seen her as a mother figure in fact, and her absence in Phoebe's life these past six months had left a painful hole. The kind woman had tried to call for the first few months, but Phoebe had never responded. After a while, the attempts to contact her had ceased.

Until now.

The ringtone ended and Phoebe let out the breath she had been holding, only to have the tune begin once again. Feeling awful, Phoebe let it go to voicemail. She would deal with the message another day, when she felt stronger. Everything felt too unsettled right now to pretend to Ida that she was fine. The woman had always had a way of seeing through her and straight to the truth of her feelings. Much the same as her son had.

Flashes of him popped up uninvited, as they so often did. Their short marriage had been happy until the devastation of loss which was followed a few months later by the stand-off associated with their long-term plans. Neither had been prepared to back down or compromise on their own career aspirations. Phoebe couldn't understand why she should give in, simply because she was the female in the relationship. He had argued it had nothing to do with that, and everything to do with the fact that he had a definite job offer, in a country which would take her nearer her goal, whilst Phoebe only had a submitted proposal and a prayer.

Nevertheless, she hadn't stopped loving him, even amidst their arguments and frustration with each other. Indeed, whilst the days were often spent in silent denial or open animosity, the nights were filled with their need to make the most of every last second together. As the day of his departure loomed, and his packing began to take up the corners of their small apartment, they had clung to each other in the dark hours, when no words needed to be spoken and their bodies could say what their stubborn minds could not.

Even to the last minute, he had hoped that Phoebe would change her mind. She herself hadn't even been sure that she wouldn't. Then suddenly he was gone, their home was eerily silent, and Phoebe had mentally closed the door on that chapter in her life. It was just a shame that her heart hadn't got the memo.

ELEVEN

At four on the dot, the doorbell rang and Phoebe let herself out to meet Jack. She couldn't deny that she had taken extra time getting ready, opting for a long skirt and ankle boots rather than her usual jeans, and wearing a bit of make-up to try to hide the fact that she had spent much of the afternoon crying. The pent-up emotions of the past few months had all been released, triggered by seeing her mother-in-law's name on her phone screen.

Phoebe could still remember how her husband smelt, how his voice had a certain low timbre that she could recognise anywhere, how it felt to be held in his arms as their hearts beat in frantic unison after their lovemaking. Suddenly, it had all been too painful – the memories, the cloying regret – until Phoebe had given in to her feelings in a way that she had steadfastly refused up until now.

Never mind, having hopefully purged the emotions and cleansed herself of their hold on her, Phoebe was looking forward to her time with Jack. He seemed to have smartened up for the occasion too – his beard was neatly trimmed, and he wore beige chinos and a shirt beneath a navy jacket. Phoebe smiled and held out his fleece coat.

"Thank you," he took the proffered item of clothing and offered her his arm. Phoebe linked her arm in his, thinking how old-fashioned and charming he was, as they walked down the front path together.

"No Oscar?" she asked, half teasing.

"No, I thought we might go somewhere a bit more peaceful tonight, and they don't allow dogs. I hope that's okay?" he paused as they reached the street and looked at her earnestly, hesitantly.

"Of course!" Phoebe gently squeezed the arm which she held, and lost herself for a moment in his grey eyes. They were an unusual shade – neither blue nor a full grey – and more than that, they held a light and a warmth which drew her in. Jack looked at her just as intently, his face inching closer, dipping down until she could feel his breath on her face. Just as Phoebe thought he might close the distance and kiss her, and unsure herself how she would feel about that, he seemed to snap back to reality and pulled away quickly.

"Yes, excellent, my car is just around the corner."

"Oh, are we leaving St. Andrews?"

"Not far, just along to a small village called Ceres. There's a new fish restaurant there. I should have texted you to ask, but I didn't have your number," he paused, floundering for the right words. Phoebe had expected them just to go for another drink, not a whole meal, but she nodded her agreement, aware suddenly of the butterflies in her stomach at the thought of spending the whole evening in this man's company. It was a very long time since she'd been on a date with anyone new.

"That sounds lovely, Jack," she whispered, wondering for a brief second if this was too much, too soon. However, she had to move on sometime, and Phoebe decided to go with the flow for once.

The restaurant had been beautiful. They had sat for

drinks on the small patio terrace, before taking a table inside for an early evening meal. Their conversation had flowed just as easily as the night before, and Phoebe had laughed more than at any other time that year. She felt relaxed and happy, and hardly recognised the woman she saw smiling back at her in the bathroom mirror.

"It's only seven-thirty," she said when she returned to the table, having come to a decision on her way back, "perhaps we could go for a walk on the beach?"

"Perfect," Phoebe was rewarded with a huge grin, "it's my favourite place! Do you mind if we drop home to collect Oscar, as he'll be needing a walk, then we could wander down to West Sands?"

"I love that beach," Phoebe replied, "it's been my second home since I got here! Of course, by all means bring Oscar along!"

They split the bill and walked out of the restaurant onto the quiet country street. It was still light, and the birds were vociferous in the trees above their heads. When she felt Jack's hand reach out and touch hers as they walked the short distance to the car, Phoebe accepted the contact he silently offered, taking his hand in hers and feeling the electricity which shot up her arm at the feel of his skin on hers. As the car came in sight, Phoebe felt the small touch of Jack's thumb moving against her palm. She didn't want to break the contact, and felt suddenly emotional, the waves of feeling from earlier in the day assailing her once more. She chastised herself silently for being a fool, both for looking continually backwards, and for having such a heady response to a tiny bit of physical affection. When she looked up at Jack as they reached the car, however, Phoebe realised that he, too, seemed thoughtful and it crossed her mind that they should probably discuss where they both stood in terms of relationships before this progressed any farther. After all, they had both skirted the subject so far.

For now, though, caught in the moment as she was, all Phoebe could do was smile up at him and whisper, "it was such a lovely meal, thank you."

"Everything about it was perfect," he responded, his hold on her hand tightening briefly before Jack let go to move around to his own door, leaving Phoebe blushing and her hand feeling cold now it no longer held his warmth.

TWELVE

Jack seemed to hesitate too long at his front door, as if he was contemplating what to do with Phoebe, and she shifted from foot to foot awkwardly. Eventually, he invited her to wait inside while he changed out of his smart clothes. Of course, the moment Oscar heard the key in the front door, he was jumping to meet them, nearly knocking Phoebe flying as he pushed passed Jack and launched himself at her on the small path.

"So sorry!" Jack muttered, trying to grab the dog's collar, "I swear, he's like Houdini, I've no idea how he gets out of his crate. He's always settled inside and the door shut before I come out!"

"No matter," Phoebe said, wiping the dog slobber from

her skirt and following them into the house.

The décor was elegant and welcoming, but most definitely chosen by a man, Phoebe thought to herself as she sat and waited in the small sitting room. There were no homely touches and the colour palette was dark and muted. Why she should feel relieved at no evidence of a woman in his personal space, she refused to acknowledge to herself, in denial as Phoebe was with regard to her growing interest in the man. *You've known him a day! Pull yourself together!* Phoebe was giving herself a stern internal talking to as Jack reappeared, looking just as attractive in his jeans as he had in his smart trousers.

He must surely have a cleaner, though, she noted, as there was not a spot of dust anywhere, nor anything seemingly out of place – no stray coffee cups or books, nothing. *Had he expected to bring her back?*

"Would you like a glass of wine before we go back out?" Jack ran his hand through his short-cropped hair, and Phoebe caught the nervousness coming off him in waves.

Her heart lurched at the sight of him, and she wanted nothing more in that moment than to walk over and put her arms around his waist, drawing him close and feeling the anxiety drain away from them both.

Instead, she sat where she was and said, "That would be lovely, thank you."

Jack disappeared back into the hallway, and Phoebe couldn't resist following him to get a look at another room in the house. The kitchen was long and narrow, a galley shape which was sparsely furnished and minimalist in design. It matched the starkness of the room she had just left, and Phoebe couldn't help but feel that the décor was at odds with the warmth of the man who had chatted with her so easily at both the bar and the restaurant. She accepted the large glass of red gratefully and watched as Jack busied himself putting on plastic gloves to add food to Oscar's bowl, before removing them again once the task was complete. He then washed his hands and dried them, the same cleaning process three times in a row. After ensuring the remaining cans of dog food were all facing with their labels forward on the small shelf next to the dog crate, he finally came to stand opposite her.

"Are you okay?" Phoebe couldn't help herself, his change in demeanour was so noticeable.

"Ahh, yes, sorry, thanks," Jack stumbled over his words, "I'm just not used to having anyone in my space… in my house, I mean. You're the first in a long while!"

"Oh, I see," though Phoebe wasn't sure that she really did understand. Why would a lovely man like this not have a wide circle of friends? He was sociable and kind, what was he hiding that Phoebe didn't know about? A small seed of doubt and mistrust took root in her mind, though her physical reaction to him could not be denied.

"Shall we go through to the lounge?" he asked, turning and leading her back to the room she had just left. Oscar quickly wolfed down the food in his bowl and trotted along after her. Jack let Phoebe choose a seat first, so she sat on the end of a large, three-seater, black leather sofa, watching as he deliberated where he himself should sit. The internal battle was seemingly won and Jack lowered himself onto the same sofa, though at the other end to Phoebe.

A small silence engulfed them as they both took sips of their wine, and Phoebe wondered where the easy conversation had gone.

"Do you teach from home?"

"Tell me more about your albatrosses…!"

They both laughed as they began speaking at once.

"Sorry!" Jack grinned and was transformed back to the

man she had first met. "Yes, I have a teaching room off the hallway out there. It's the only room my students enter when they're here. I can cope with that." He stopped short, looking uncomfortable, as if he had said too much.

Phoebe smiled gently, "You have a lovely home," she sought to reassure him and put him more at ease. "As for the albatrosses, well I could bore you with details of them for hours!" Phoebe explained about the research on the island of Laysan with the United States Fish and Wildlife Service, which she had proposed in her grant application, and by the time she had stopped talking their drinks were finished. At the sight of Jack standing, Oscar jumped up from his spot against Phoebe's legs, his tail wagging in anticipation.

"I'll just wash these," Jack said, disappearing off in the direction of the kitchen. Phoebe thought it a little strange, as she would have left their glasses on the coffee table till later, but she simply nodded at his retreating form. It was obvious that Jack liked everything just so.

Once Oscar was on his lead, his excitement had reached fever pitch, and no-one got through the doorway without numerous doggy kisses and jumps onto their chest. Phoebe giggled as she wiped his lick from her cheek and they set off towards the beach. There was no chance for holding hands this time, as Jack was dragged ahead of her on the narrow pavement by his eager canine companion, leaving Phoebe to hurry along in their wake.

＊

THIRTEEN

The sun was just setting as they made their way onto West Sands, and apart from a few others a way off, there was no-one else as far as the eye could see. Oscar sprinted away as soon as his cumbersome leash was unhooked, and Jack straightened up from the action, looking at Phoebe as he did so.

"Such a beautiful night," he exclaimed, giving her an easy smile, "I love being out here. It's as if everything which preoccupies my mind… everything which drives me mad… disappears behind the sound of the waves and the embrace of nature." He blushed at his own honesty, at the emotion in his voice which some men may have tried to hide, or perhaps would not have spoken of the feeling at all.

"Me too," Phoebe moved to his side and found his hand, taking it in hers and rubbing her thumb along the seam where his palm met his wrist. She desperately wanted to enquire more about the things that drove him mad, perhaps in the hope of sharing some of her own demons, but they were still too strange to each other for her to have the confidence to do so. Instead, they simply resumed their walk along the beach, laughing when they saw Oscar romping in the waves.

"I always forget to bring a towel," Jack groaned, "It's like having a toddler who won't listen to direction!"

"Do you have any children?" the question was out before Phoebe could catch it back. After all, he was a man in his thirties, he could already be separated as she was, divorced even, or have children of his own.

Jack paused and faced her thoughtfully, "No, ah, I haven't been blessed in that department yet. Have you?"

"Me?" her voice went up an octave and her stomach lurched, as if she hadn't expected him to return the question, "No, none, though I was, I mean, I am, ah married," Phoebe froze, she hadn't intended the information to come out either at this moment or indeed so bluntly as it had. She had no experience of sharing this particular fact with anyone, let alone in a romantic context.

"You're married?" It came out louder than he intended, and Jack seemed to turn a deep shade of red.

"Well, separated, I should say, the past six months," she added quickly.

Jack let out an audible breath, "Ah, okay."

"Are you? Separated from anyone?" Phoebe asked cautiously.

"No, I, er, have never had the pleasure of settling down with someone. In fact my last serious relationship was several years ago," the heat in his face was flaming now and Phoebe felt the need to reach out and comfort him. Why he had been single for so long she had no idea, though perhaps his reluctance to have people into his home was a clue. It was so long since Phoebe had been in the dating game, that she had forgotten what it was like to not know a partner inside and out. She had no idea what skeletons hid in Jack's closet, and he was hardly likely to expose them to her after knowing each other for just a couple of days. Choosing to avoid any more inquisitions, she reached out a tentative hand and laid it on his chest, palm flat down over his jacket. Even through the layers of clothing, she could feel Jack's heart beating erratically.

"Hey," she whispered to soothe him, just as Oscar chose that moment to jump up for their attention, spraying them with sea water and nearly knocking Phoebe off balance. Jack caught her elbow and drew her towards him so that she did not fall, and they stood there, frozen in time.

"Woah! I've got you," he whispered, his eyes burning a path into hers, his brow creased into a frown. Whether it was worry for what they'd disclosed, or for her potentially taking a tumble, Phoebe wasn't sure. To Oscar, he shouted, "Bad dog!" though the pup was too far away by now to hear or to heed.

They were so close now, her chest pressed up against his, her original hand trapped between them, and he holding her other arm. Silently, Jack ran his hand down from her elbow to her hand and back up again, and Phoebe reacted to his touch.

"I haven't met anyone like you before," Jack whispered, "not someone who grabs my attention, who I feel… a connection to."

Phoebe couldn't say the same, as her connection to her ex-husband had been electric since the moment they had met. Nor, though, could she deny she did not feel a certain chemistry with Jack either.

"There is definitely a... connection," she admitted. Their faces were almost touching now, as neither had pulled back from the strange embrace, and both had to lean in to hear the other over the crashing of the waves next to them. It was almost dark now and they should be heading back. Instead, the invisible string which connected them seemed to draw their faces even closer, until it would take hardly any movement at all for them to kiss. Yet Jack made no move, and Phoebe felt suddenly very unsure of herself. Her self-confidence, since the separation, had been very low.

So, they simply hovered there, in what was now an awkward intimacy, until Phoebe pulled away. Avoiding Jack's eyes, she said, "I should be heading back."

"Of course," his voice sounded sad, and Phoebe also felt a melancholy which she did not want to examine too closely. For a few moments, she had wished she was here with her husband, imagining how he would have scooped her up and pretended to throw her into the waves, how he would have run his hands through her hair, held her face and kissed her as if it might be their last ever kiss. And yet, here she was with someone else entirely, and their last ever kiss had come and gone already. Phoebe felt the emotion rise into her throat and fought to hold back the tears, as Jack chased

Oscar, who was reluctant to join them on the walk back.

Phoebe felt impatient to return home, to her own company, where she could analyse her conflicting emotions and perhaps give in to them privately. Jack had done nothing wrong, of course, he could not be held responsible for her sudden shift, and Phoebe wondered if it wasn't just too soon to be trying to fill a hole that was still the shape of one particular man.

FOURTEEN

After a quick and awkwardly formal goodnight at her gate, Phoebe rushed the last short distance up her path, glad Jack had not walked her to the door. Citing a need to bath Oscar as his excuse, the man had seemed plainly uncomfortable. Phoebe was aware that she was not exactly giving off welcoming vibes herself, having retreated into her shell for the full walk back from the beach. As she entered the apartment, to the loud ballads of Celine Dion – a favourite of Mel's and not to her own taste – Mel heard her mobile ringing in her handbag. Scrabbling around inside the random contents, she eventually found the device, just as the ring tone stopped.

"Ooh ten o'clock, who's a dirty stop-out then!" Mel's

cheery teasing was ignored as Phoebe finally located her phone, unsettled when she saw Ida's number again.

"Huh?" Phoebe glanced up in irritation.

"Oh don't mind me! I was just wondering how your date with John went?"

"It's Jack and it was… a game of two halves! Hang on a mo while I check my messages!" Phoebe knew she could put it off no longer. She had four missed calls and three messages from her mother-in-law now and the realisation suddenly hit her that perhaps something had happened to her ex. Her hands shaking, her heart in overdrive, Phoebe called her voicemail service. The most recent of the messages came through first.

"Phoebe, Phoebe dear, I'm sorry to pester you so much, but it's George, he's in a bad way lass, he's in the hospital in Perth, his heart you see…" Phoebe could hear beeping and machines in the background and the muffled tones of Ida's voice, as if she had recently been crying, cut through Phoebe's shock at the news. George had always been a jovial, robust man. Golfing, gardening, always outdoors. Phoebe knew he had a heart condition but thought it was well controlled. She hit the call-back button before she could talk herself out of it – now wasn't the time to be selfish.

"Hello?" The voice on the other end sounded frail and nothing like the woman Phoebe knew.

"Ida? It's Phoebe, I got your messages. Sorry that I didn't…"

"Phoebe lass! Thank you, thank you for calling back. I'm just getting in the car to pop home for a shower. Do you want to meet me there?"

"Oh, I, well, yes, I suppose…" Phoebe didn't know what she'd intended when she'd made the call – to offer some support probably – but it wasn't driving the hour to Perth late at night to see a woman she hadn't had contact with for over half a year. Phoebe didn't actually know what the sweet couple had been told about the break-up by their son. Nevertheless, the hope and relief in Ida's voice touched Phoebe and she found she couldn't refuse. "Yes, let me quickly get changed and I'll set off right away. I should be there after eleven."

"Thank you, see you soon then," Ida ended the call before Phoebe could respond, nor even enquire as to exactly how George was faring. She hoped she could find their home in the darkness. She had been there many times, but had never been the driver. She wasn't sure what, if anything, her going there would achieve or help with, but Phoebe gave Mel a quick recap before trudging up the stairs to change and pack an overnight bag.

The journey up through Dundee and then along the A90 had been thankfully quiet and without incident, as Phoebe's nerves were on edge from the bad news she'd received. It must be very serious, she decided, if Ida wanted her there straight away. It only now crossed her mind, that of course he must have been told. She wondered if her husband was on his way, if he'd found someone new in their time apart, someone to comfort him the way she would have in the past. Making a conscious effort to shift such thoughts from her mind, Phoebe drove into the small cul-de-sac with relief. Her parents-in-law had the house in the far corner, where Phoebe could see the porch light was on. Ida's small Skoda sat in the driveway, with another, larger car behind, so Phoebe parked on the street curb outside.

Retrieving her bag from the boot, Phoebe made her way up the path, and rang the doorbell. The clanging chimes of 'Consider Yourself' from the musical 'Oliver' began playing inside. It was just like George and Ida to choose something so ridiculous and funny and Phoebe was smiling to herself when the door opened.

"Phoebs?" The surprise in the very masculine voice was evident. More than surprise, shock even. A voice Phoebe would know anywhere.

"Hello Mark, I didn't realise you were here."

"Of course I'm here, my dad is seriously ill. Why are you here?"

"Your mum called me and asked me to come straight up, she didn't mention you..." Phoebe trailed off as it occurred to her that perhaps Ida had deliberately omitted some information when speaking to them both. Vital information at that.

Mark tried to hide his confusion at seeing his beautiful wife again. *Ex-wife*, he reminded himself morosely. The last thing he'd expected when he'd driven Mum back from the hospital, leaving Uncle Alan to sit with Dad for a bit, was to see Phoebe on the doorstep. How had she come from Oxford so quickly?

"Ah, come in then," he muttered, knowing he was being extremely rude, but having seen his dad attached to all those wires and machines, and now this, he'd had all the shocks he could take for one day. He closed the door behind Phoebe, getting a waft of the familiar perfume as she walked past him into the hallway. It was all he could to keep his hands to himself and not reach out for her, for the hug he'd needly so badly since he'd arrived. Since they'd split up in fact. Instead, Mark simply motioned Phoebe into the sitting room as if she were a mere acquaintance of the family come to ask after his father, and followed her sombrely into the room.

FIFTEEN

"I didn't expect you to be here…I mean I knew you would come, I just didn't think I'd run into you…" Phoebe knew she was gabbling. She was wringing her hands together in her lap, still wearing her coat, with her overnight bag perched on the floor beside her. She wasn't sure whether to stand up again and hug Mark, or run for the car while she still had her emotions somewhat in check. Looking up at him, at his gaunt, pale face, she wondered when he had last eaten. The change in him could not be from this weekend alone, she thought. Certainly, he would be tired and perhaps had missed several meals, as well as having had a terrible shock, but you don't lose twenty pounds or so overnight. Phoebe wondered suddenly if she herself

70

looked different since their split. Not that she could ask him, of course.

The awkward silence was broken by Ida rushing into the room, her short, grey hair still wet.

"Aw, Phoebe, there you are lass, I knew you'd come. I could certainly do with one of your famous hugs, we all could," the woman flashed a pointed look at her son, before taking Phoebe, who had risen to stand beside them, in a huge cuddle. Ida was only just five feet tall, so came up to Phoebe's shoulder where she stood at five foot nine. Phoebe wrapped her arms around the lady who seemed so much tinier than she remembered, before pulling away. Ida looked expectantly between the two, until eventually Mark stepped forward and opened his arms to Phoebe. For Ida's sake she said nothing and walked into the offered embrace. Without thought, her head fit snugly on the dip of his shoulder where it always had, her arms wound around his waist and she pulled him tightly to her. Embarrassingly close, Phoebe realised too late, and felt her cheeks flame red. It was so familiar, so comforting as if she had come home, that the tears came too quickly for Phoebe to put a halt to them. She had no choice but to let them flow, wetting Mark's shirt. After too long, much too long for simple friends, they pulled away, and Phoebe tried to wipe her face.

Nothing got by the sharp-eyed Ida, however, who assumed Phoebe was upset about George.

"Aw there, lassie, he's in the best place. The doctor's said that since it's been over twenty-four hours the chances are reducing that he'll have another cardiac arrest right away."

Phoebe chanced a glance at Mark, whose eyes also shone glassy in the low light from the lamp in the room. Clearly, he had been affected too, but Ida was correct, he could just be upset about his Dad, understandably so, and the small bit of affection had likely caused his emotions to bubble over. Phoebe wasn't totally convinced however, as Mark's eyes had the look of a man confused, a mixture of longing and regret, their intensity so strong that Phoebe had to look away lest she stand staring into them and embarrass herself even further.

"Do we need to be getting back to the hospital?" Mark directed the question at his mother, his voice suddenly rough and croaky.

"Aye son, we do, I'll just go and dry my hair and fill a flask with tea, I can't stand that hospital lukewarm machine stuff. You can just drop me off though, only one allowed overnight, then you and Phoebe can come back in the morning."

Phoebe was confused. Was it not the whole point of the late night trip that she should see George now in case the worst happened?

"Er, did you not want me to, I mean, where should I..?" Phoebe asked, feeling Mark's eyes boring into the side of her cheek as she faced Ida.

"Not tonight dear, I thought you could stay here and keep Mark company."

"Mum I don't need…" Ida cut him off before Mark could say anything else in protest.

"Hush, lad, you may pretend you don't need her, but she's here now, and I can see how close the two of you still are. You just drop me off at the hospital and come along in the morning together."

There was no arguing in any way that would not upset the woman whose husband lay in a hospital bed. Nothing for it, but to agree now and then discuss it between themselves when Mark returned. Phoebe had no intention of staying the night in the house alone with him, but it was after midnight and her options were limited. She would have to think fast while he was on the short trip to the hospital.

Phoebe busied herself in the kitchen while Mark was gone, anything to keep her mind from dwelling and her heart from brooding on the unexpected reunion with her estranged husband. She made a pot of coffee to keep them going, as she felt sleep might be a long shot in the current circumstances, and was just pouring two cups when she heard his key in the door. The nerves in her stomach came to life once more, and Phoebe asked herself for the dozenth time what she was actually doing here. It was too late at night to disappear now, though, so she carried the cups through to the sitting room with a look of resignation.

"All okay?" she asked from habit, as she entered the room.

"Aye, I made sure she got to the ward safely. There's no bed, she'll have to rest in the chair. I should have stayed and let my mother rest here, but she insisted, she just wants to be with him," Mark paused as Phoebe handed him the hot cup and looked at her intently, as if his words had brought other thoughts to mind.

"Well, he's in the best place. I'm so glad he's over the scariest time now," Phoebe spoke softly, sitting in the big armchair next to the fireplace. Mark sat on the sofa, at the end nearest to her, perched on the edge in what looked like an uncomfortable position.

This will be a long night, Phoebe thought to herself, as the awkward silence engulfed them once again.

SIXTEEN

When Mark eventually spoke, there was an odd edge to his voice, which Phoebe couldn't pinpoint – neither regret not anger, it was simply cold and distant.

"So, how are you here so quickly from Oxford then, I'm guessing you didn't just travel all the way here from the North Pacific?"

"Oxford?" Phoebe was confused, until she remembered he would have no reason to have been told of her plans, "No, my post there ended as planned with no other position offered to replace it, but my, ah, research grant to travel to the Hawaiian islands hasn't materialised yet, so I'm living down the road in St. Andrews with a six month tenure at the Scottish

Oceans Institute now. I start on Monday actually."

"St. Andrews? I didn't know they did research on albatrosses there?" His tone was almost sarcastic now, and Phoebe bit her tongue on the retort which sprang to mind. She knew that Mark really wanted to pass comment on how she had given up going to America with him, turned her back on their relationship, pinning her hope on an opportunity which had not yet come through.

Instead she simply replied, "No, it's seal populations actually," turning her head away so that she wouldn't see the accusation or scorn on his face, and he wouldn't see the disappointment on hers. When she looked back, however, Mark simply looked distressed. Even worse than when she had first arrived. The urge to go to him, to sit next to him on the settee was so strong, that Phoebe gripped her cup in both hands tightly, willing herself not to move towards him.

Mark looked as if he were about to say something several times, but each time nothing came out. Finally, he whispered harshly, "I left you behind, only because I didn't want to stand in the way of your ambition and career – they were clearly more important to you than me. But to hear that it didn't come to pass, and I lost you for nothing, after all we had been through…!" His voice raised at that last part, and Phoebe winced slightly. Her indignation rose to match her disappointment, and she simply stared at him.

When Phoebe didn't grace Mark with a response, he carried on unchecked, no longer in any way cool or detached, "You let me leave without a word, you cut all contact, you broke my heart, Phoebs!" his voice cracked at the sound of her name on his tongue, and Mark stood up quickly, slamming his cup down on the table and stalking out of the room.

Phoebe waited a moment, trying to gather her thoughts. They couldn't leave the conversation there, she decided, so she followed Mark into the dining room where he stood in a dim corner, scraping his hands through his hair. He had grown a short beard since he'd left for America, and it somehow gave him the air of being more haggard, more desperate than even his eyes alluded to. Phoebe paused in the doorway, unsure whether to approach him, before chiding herself – Mark had never been aggressive or violent towards her, bad tempered occasionally, angry rarely, so she should not fear him. That being said, she didn't really know the man who stood in front of her now, so Phoebe decided to tread carefully.

Standing about a foot from Mark, she reached out a tentative hand and touched his arm, "I should have let you know when my plans fell through. I should have asked whether you were settled in the States, I just thought it would hurt us both to keep in contact when we were still so raw from the break-up."

He lifted his eyes to hers, not stepping away from the small contact she offered, "I've missed you Phoebs!" It was said in a harsh, low tone filled with an accusation which sliced through Phoebe straight to her heart.

She wasn't sure that admitting she had felt the same was at all useful, but her mouth had spoken the words, before Phoebe's head had thought it through fully, "I've missed you too, so much. It's like part of me has been missing!" The sob that followed tore through her so quickly and shocked Phoebe by both its speed and its volume. In a second, Mark had closed the distance between them, pulling her against his chest and wrapping his arms around her. Phoebe held him just as closely, until there was no air between their bodies, feeling his breath on her head as he kissed her hair. The tears streamed down her face, and she heard his own emotional release above her.

"Phoebe, Phoebe, Phoebe," Mark whispered, as if he were assuring himself she was really there and not just a figment of his imagination.

The electricity which she had always felt when he touched her, coursed through Phoebe. Her body, seemingly starved of a catalyst until now, roared back to life. She felt Mark's touch right to her core, even though they were separated by layers of clothes and he had yet to kiss her anywhere but her head. She nuzzled her cheek against his shirt, tasting the salt of her own tears, until Phoebe felt her husband's finger under her chin, lifting her head gently to face him.

"I've missed you so much. My life has been empty without you," Mark whispered through his own tears, his words almost an accusation. Phoebe could feel his body shaking in her arms. He was certainly thinner, but more than that, this Mark seemed to be an entirely more fragile version of the strong, confident man she had known. Whereas once she'd felt that they knew each other inside and out, that they could predict each other's thoughts and actions – whilst still being individually strong and independent – Phoebe felt like she was adrift now. Completely at sea, without a map.

"I'm here now, honey," she whispered back, hating how woefully inadequate that sounded. Yet, she couldn't promise him more than this moment.

Mark rested his forehead against hers, and they stood

swaying silently. Phoebe wondered if he would kiss her. She knew that would be a bad idea, for both of them, but in that moment it was all she could think about. The feel of his lips against hers, him claiming her mouth the way he had in the past.

SEVENTEEN

Mark tried to take control of his thoughts, as so many things rushed through his mind, demanding his attention in the same moment. It was almost impossible to untangle the mess of emotions – anger, frustration, worry, anguish, hope, joy – they all vied for top place. His senses reeled to have Phoebe in his arms again, something which he had all but given up on ever happening. As annoyed as he was that his mother had gone behind his back and invited Phoebe to support him, he couldn't deny that he needed her. In fact, it scared him how much he needed this woman right now. He wanted to put some space between them, but couldn't bear to end the embrace.

Eventually, it was Phoebe who pulled back, wiping her

cheeks on the sleeve of her top and looking at him with watery eyes. The choice suddenly seemed simple to Mark – take her mouth with his and to hell with the consequences, or deliberately push her away and deal with the pain. He wasn't thinking at all clearly, and the words erupted from his mouth in a mixture of jealousy and harmful curiosity.

"So, have you found yourself a golfer, then?"

Phoebe blinked rapidly at the change in tone and direction. The spell he had cast over her was thankfully broken, and she bit back indignantly, "What? In the two weeks I've been there? Don't be ridiculous! Besides, you know how much I dislike the sport! All those times your dad offered to teach me…" A strange desire to stick the knife back into him arose in her, and she added, "It's hardly like I fit in. Mel is still living the single life. I've moved to a town where I have no interest in the sport it's famous for. Nor am I a student at its renowned university! Mind you, I have met someone, but it's still very new…"

Her words had the desired effect and Mark's face crumpled, so that Phoebe had to turn her face away, the instant regret causing a sickening ache in her stomach.

"I see."

"Have you met someone special?" she countered. Phoebe really couldn't stop herself now. Besides, the need to know, to feed the green-eyed monster which raised its ugly head at the thought of him being with someone else, was too strong an urge to fight in her sensitive state.

Mark looked at her with that intense gaze once more, apparently mulling over what he would say. Phoebe held her breath, not that she had any rights any more. No longer did she have any claim to him. Still, she could not bear the thought of him with anyone new.

Mark wanted to lie, for his own ego's sake, and to protect the tiny bit of pride that remained in him. He just could not do it. What was the point in pretending?

"No," it was said quickly and without further explanation. He turned away from Phoebe and left the room, going back to the lounge to retrieve her overnight bag.

"I'll get you settled in the guest room," Mark spoke over his shoulder, avoiding eye contact with his wife.

Phoebe had followed him and stood in the doorway. Mark's parents lived in a bungalow, with the loft converted to a guest bedroom.

"Where will you sleep?" she certainly didn't intend it to sound like an invitation, but one look at Mark told her he needed to rest just as much, if not more so than she did.

"I'll be fine on the settee here," he still would not look directly at her.

"Don't be silly! It's not like we haven't shared a bed before! Besides, you look exhausted," without thinking, Phoebe reached her hand out and cupped his cheek. They both froze, the contact sending shockwaves through them. Her thumb rubbed across his cheekbone, and Mark leaned into the touch for a brief moment.

"Whatever, it's late!" he said harshly, pulling away and striding past her and up the small staircase, leaving Phoebe feeling the coldness of his retreat.

EIGHTEEN

The loft room seemed smaller than Phoebe remembered. The bed itself was not a full double, rather a three-quarters size. Of course, this had never bothered them on visits in the past, the added intimacy often leading to several middle-of-the-night bouts of lovemaking. Now, though, sharing the small space seemed a daunting prospect. Phoebe disappeared into the tiny en suite, leaving Mark to decide how he wanted to proceed. When she returned, he was lying on top of the covers, in his usual spot on the left of the bed, wearing his underwear and t-shirt. He had his back to the rest of the room, and Phoebe turned off the lamp, slipping under the covers with her back also to him.

The strange cuckoo-clock on the wall, which they'd often joked about in the past – a relic of Mark's parents' honeymoon in Switzerland – ticked loudly, as if mocking Phoebe's attempts to sleep. Despite her body's exhaustion, her mind was whirring ceaselessly, and her senses were all at full alert. Having Mark so close, albeit on top of the duvet, did strange things to her. She could feel his back pressed up against hers, feel his breathing and warmth against her. Phoebe desperately wanted to turn around and reach out to him, even though her head told her it was possibly the most stupid thing she could do right now. Nevertheless, she could tell by his breathing and how tense his back muscles were, that Mark wasn't asleep either and that fuelled her need to be closer to him.

"Are you awake?" It was Mark who spoke first, his voice a rough whisper.

"Umhm," Phoebe gave a non-committal response, though her heart rejoiced that he had asked the question.

"Come here," it was a demand not a request, and Phoebe felt Mark behind her roll onto his back. She turned to face him and saw his arm outstretched along the pillow behind her. Without speaking, Phoebe moved against him. She lay on her side facing him, against his torso and with her head back in the nook of Mark's shoulder. He brought his arm down around her back, snuggling her closer against him, and Phoebe felt him sigh against her hair. It felt strange with her beneath the covers, and him on top of them, so Phoebe lifted the blanket in invitation. Mark pulled away for a moment to join her underneath, before returning to the same position. It felt intimate, despite their nightwear, and both old and new at the same time. Phoebe's hand itched to run across his chest the way she used to. She wanted to feel the new addition of a beard across his jaw, and reach up to his face. Instead she lay her arm across his stomach, her hand reaching the tiny bit of mattress on the other side.

"That's better," Mark's voice was so low and quiet that Phoebe felt it more as a rumble against her head.

"Yes," she whispered, not trusting herself to say more.

"Try to get some sleep. I love you," they both stiffened the moment he'd said the words. Both knew it was out of habit, yet a sudden awkwardness prevailed.

"You too," Phoebe whispered, trying to put him back at ease. She did not expand on whether she referred to the sleep or the declaration, but she snuggled down into him and felt Mark's body relax in response.

Phoebe was groggily aware of a strange trilling sound coming from nearby. She moved to sit up, but her legs were entwined with someone else's and for a moment she struggled to recall where she was. She knew it was Mark whose chest she was lying half-across, of course. Who else would it be but her husband? Suddenly he sat bolt upright, and Phoebe had to move quickly to accommodate his new position. Mark fumbled on the bedside table next to him, flicking on the lamp and grabbing his phone which was guilty of making the noise which awoke them.

"Hello?" Mark's voice was almost slurred, thick with sleep. Phoebe could not hear the full conversation on the other side of the call, but gathered it was urgent when Mark jumped out of bed and started trying to put on his trousers, the phone lodged under his ear. Seeing him, Phoebe also got up and rushed into the bathroom where she had left her clothes over the radiator. Getting dressed, she could tell that it was Ida who had called, and from the sound of things it was not good news.

"I have to go," Mark said as she returned to the bedroom, shoving his phone in his pocket and running his hands through his hair.

"Okay, I'll come," there was no question in it, but that Phoebe would go with him, "I'll drive. You can tell me on the way." There was no argument this time, no debate.

"Thanks," Mark's hand was shaking, and Phoebe took hold of it and led him down the narrow staircase.

NINETEEN

The hospital corridors seemed deserted as Phoebe and Mark rushed through them. His message from his mother had been garbled, interspersed with sobbing, but Mark had gotten the gist that his dad had suffered another cardiac arrest. Finally arriving at ward five, the coronary care unit, Mark rushed to the nurses' station to enquire where he could find his dad. Before he could speak to someone, however, Ida appeared, her face drawn and wet, and rushed into her son's arms.

"Marl, Mark lad, your father, he's…" she paused as if unable to say the words.

"Is he still in the same room as earlier?" Mark's reply was spoken over his shoulder, as he strode away towards the bay, leaving Ida and Phoebe standing.

"He's gone, lass," Ida sobbed against Phoebe's shoulder. Phoebe took the woman into her arms and rubbed her back soothingly, whilst worrying what Mark was about to see.

"Oh, Ida, I'm so, so sorry. Let's go and find Mark," Phoebe already felt the loss of the older man who had been so kind to her throughout her marriage. Ida suddenly became aware that her son was no longer with them and they both hurried in the direction of George's room.

The sight which greeted them shook Phoebe more than anything she could recall in her past. Mark was sitting in the chair beside his father's bed, sobbing over the chest of the man who was no longer aware.

"It was so sudden. He had another attack, and I called you while they worked on him, then it was over, and he was gone," Ida was wailing now, and Phoebe was torn whether to comfort the woman, or go to the man whose heart was breaking at the bedside.

"Why, why Dad, I needed to talk to you. I needed to say goodbye…" Mark's private thoughts tumbled out of him.

Phoebe settled Ida in the large wingback chair in the corner of the bay with a blanket over her – the woman was sobbing silently now and evidently in shock – and went to stand at Mark's side, rubbing her hand in patterns on his back. She wasn't sure he was even aware of her presence, until Mark brought one of his arms up and circled it around her waist, pulling her close and leaning his head against Phoebe's stomach. His face was ashen, and the tears rolled down and dripped onto her top. Phoebe held him to her, running her fingers through his hair and down his back. She leant forwards and spoke against his head, not really aware of what she was saying, just words of comfort which sprang to mind.

After a while, Ida stood and went to the other side of the bed, whispering to George and kissing his face, so Phoebe encouraged Mark to move away and give his parents some private time. Reluctantly, Mark stood and allowed himself to be led into the corridor.

"I'm sorry, I'm so sorry, honey," Phoebe whispered, crying softly. She opened her arms and Mark walked into them without hesitation, leaning his head down to nuzzle his face into her neck. He said nothing, but Phoebe felt each of his sobs tearing through him as his body trembled in her arms. She rubbed the back of his neck with one hand and wrapped the other arm around him tightly, desperate to offer some strength and comfort. When they saw the team coming up the corridor with a trolley to collect the body, Mark pulled away to get his mother from the room. As soon as their hug ended, though, he grabbed Phoebe's hand to bring her with him, as if that small touch was like a lifeline. As they went through the motions of watching George being taken away, and supporting Ida as best they could, Mark never broke that contact. Whether he was holding her hand or leaning against her side with his arm about her waist, Mark sought Phoebe's constant touch and reassurance. It didn't cross her mind even once not to give it. Indeed, she too needed the presence of the man who had helped her through many troubled times.

Phoebe remembered another ward almost exactly a year ago, in a different hospital, much the same as this one, where they had held each other tightly. On that occasion, though, Phoebe had been in the bed, shocked and confused as the doctor told them their sixteen-week pregnancy had come to an end. Following her cramping and bleeding they had come in to be checked over, only to find out that their baby had stopped growing at fourteen weeks. The devastation from that news had stayed with them a long time, right up until they split six months ago, and Phoebe credited the grief for fuelling part of her unremitting desire to pursue her career so steadfastly.

She fought to bring her mind back to the present. She could not support Mark now, the way he had supported her then, if she let herself be dragged back down into painful memories. He was sitting with Ida in the family room, as the consultant spoke to them in medical terms as to what had happened to George tonight. Phoebe had offered to leave, to give them some privacy, but Mark had increased his pressure on her hand slightly, and looked at her from swollen, bloodshot eyes. Of course, Phoebe wouldn't leave him now.

TWENTY

The cold morning light was shining through the windows, and the hospital was alive with the hustle and bustle of another day when the trio made their way out of the front entrance. Phoebe left Mark holding up an inconsolable Ida whilst she went to bring the car round for them. They would get her home and into bed, before beginning the job of calling family and friends. George's brother, Alan, would meet them shortly at the house, and would also help. Phoebe wondered if they should ask the local doctor to pop round and prescribe something to calm Ida and help her fall asleep, but she had yet to broach this with Mark. One thing at a time. He certainly didn't look like he could think about anything more than that, and

Phoebe's heart broke for him.

"I'll just go and get ready for morning mass," Ida, a practicing Catholic her whole life, announced as she let them into the hallway of the bungalow.

Phoebe shot a concerned look at Mark, who said softly, but firmly, "Mum, the only place you're going is to bed! Come on, let's run you a bath and get you settled."

"No, son, I need to pray, and speak to Father Michaels, and…"

"Yes, Ida, and I promise there will be plenty of time, after you've had a rest. Why don't I phone the church and let Father Michaels know of George's passing? Then he could maybe call around later," Phoebe tried to cajole the distraught woman. Ida had stopped crying when they were in the car, but her eyes had a distant look, and Phoebe knew the best place for her right now was in bed.

A few more reassurances and they finally got Ida through to the bathroom. Phoebe ran her a bath whilst Mark made a cup of tea for them all. Phoebe watched him as he walked into the kitchen and picked up the kettle, as if he was on autopilot. She would give him every ounce of comfort she could, once she had her mother-in-law settled.

They had made the first round of phone calls to family, had a visit from the doctor for Ida, who was understandably unable to settle, and had shared in their grief with Alan who had now left. Finally, Ida was asleep in her bed, and the clock showed it was already three in the afternoon. They were alone for the first time since they had received the call in the middle of the night, and Phoebe was suddenly unsure what to do or say. Mark had kept her close the whole morning and she had of course obliged. Now, the reality settled on Phoebe that she was meant to be starting a new job the next day. She had phoned Mel that morning to explain she would spend the day here, and had heard that Jack had called round to see her. Phoebe couldn't give that any headspace right now, as she had Mark and Ida to think about, and her own grief and buried trauma which the scene at the hospital had caused to resurface.

"So," Mark began, checking the time on his phone, "do you need to be going?" His tone was hopeful rather than resigned and Phoebe knew she could not leave him yet.

"Soon, probably, but not yet, I can stay with you

awhile."

"Thank you," the relief on his face was evident, despite the taught worry lines which were even more prominent today.

"Of course, honey, I know how much you're hurting," she hadn't intended the words to affect him, but they seemed to be the straw which broke the camel's back. Since their return to the bungalow that morning, Mark had managed to keep his feelings in check. Going through the motions of the list of practical arrangements they needed to think about. Now, though, the tears streamed down his cheeks and he lowered his face into his hands. Phoebe moved from where she was standing to kneel in front of him, laying his head on her shoulder and holding him to her.

"I've got you," she whispered through her own tears, "let it out, I'm here."

Mark shook with the force of his emotion, and Phoebe soothed him with her hands and her words, letting him just be. When he eventually raised his head, he sat back and motioned for Phoebe to join him. Not next to him, this time, rather he indicated the spot on his lap. It used to be Phoebe's favourite thing, to sit on her husband's knee and snuggle against his chest whilst he ran his fingers through her curls, gently untangling them. Could she do that now though, after all the water that had gone under their bridge? Should she?

One look at Mark was enough to make the decision for her. He needed this. Heck, they both needed this. She settled herself tentatively on his lap, curled up sideways with her cheek resting against him. Mark wrapped his arms around her and laid his chin on her head.

"That's better," he said, and it was.

TWENTY-ONE

Time stood still, and Phoebe had no idea how long they sat like that, both eventually dozing off. When the landline phone rang, it startled them both, and Mark dropped a quick kiss on Phoebe's forehead as he reached across to the end table to answer it. Phoebe made a move to shift off him, but Mark held her tight and the look he gave her was unmistakeable. Obliging him, Phoebe settled back against his chest. She would stay where she was while Mark took the call, then Phoebe knew she must think about leaving.

It was the priest, Father Michaels, asking if he could call around after evening mass. Phoebe looked at her watch – five-thirty. Mark thanked the man and said they'd look forward to seeing him later, before ending the call and turning back to Phoebe.

"I should wake my mum and make her something to eat before he arrives," the sadness, the deep melancholy in his voice affected Phoebe greatly, and she swallowed down the emotion which threatened to spill out once again.

"I'll make a meal for you both, for all of us, before I leave," she said.

"Really? You don't have to."

"Of course, it's no bother," they sat, so close, their faces almost touching as he bent his head forward. Phoebe felt his small sigh against her forehead.

"Thank you, Phoebs, if you hadn't been here I don't know how I'd have gotten though today…" his eyes searched hers, his voice wobbly.

Phoebe's heart beat fast in her chest. She needed to kiss him. Her whole body and soul yearned for it, but her head held them in check. Mark, too, seemed to struggle with the same affliction. Phoebe looked up at him, as his face hovered just above her. He lowered his mouth as if the battle in his mind had been won, then pulled away swiftly. Phoebe felt strangely bereft in that instant, as if something promised had been withheld.

Stupid really, she chided herself, as he had not offered to kiss her, nor had she invited it. Still, the pain was sudden and, other than the loss of George, much stronger than anything Phoebe had felt since she had arrived yesterday.

Mark clearly felt the same. A pained expression contorted his features before he quickly lowered his mouth once again, this time without pausing in his trajectory. His lips crushed against Phoebe's with a passion that caught her off guard. His tongue claimed immediate entry to her mouth and she returned his advance with equal force. A fire lit inside them, as they explored each other with hands and mouths, until eventually good sense prevailed once more and Phoebe pulled back, panting. Mark was equally breathless, his cheeks red and his breath coming in quick gasps.

"I can't apologise for that," he said, his voice gravelly, "and I won't."

"No," Phoebe said, not wanting him to say sorry, to say it was a mistake, "no, you don't have to. It's been a difficult, sad, sad day. We just needed a release, that's all." At least they had stopped before they had done anything serious, she thought, standing from his lap and offering her hand to help him up. Mark accepted her help, his brown eyes dark and brooding, his mouth turned down in displeasure. Phoebe had seen the look many times in the month before he had left for the states. Yet this time she couldn't tell if his disappointment was in her, in himself, or in them both. It may, of course, have been disappointment that they had cut off when they did, but Phoebe didn't want to dwell on that possibility.

By the time Ida had eaten from a tray in bed, and had sat for a while with Father Michaels, it was dark and late. Phoebe hadn't felt at any point that it was a suitable time to say her goodbyes, so she stayed, offering cups of tea and hugs to Ida and Mark. He had been her shadow the whole time. Whenever he knew his mum was settled, he would be back by Phoebe's side, his arm around her waist or his hand in hers. Phoebe understood the need for physical contact. They had been the same with each other after the miscarriage. Far from pushing them apart, and each grieving separately, they had become joined at the hip for a while. Crossing the road to eat lunch with each other in their respective Oxford science buildings, and spending every moment outside of work together. It had been the worst time for them as a couple, and also, perversely, one of the best. At the time, Phoebe had felt it cemented their relationship. They had only been married a year at that point, though they'd been together five years before getting hitched, having met at her second research post, in Inverness, when Phoebe was twenty-six and still struggling to get her doctorate in her niche subject. Mark had already been Dr. Ross by then, an astrophysicist and a few years older than her. He had taken Phoebe under his wing and helped her complete the work she'd needed to achieve her PhD, despite her subject of study being so removed from his own. He had been patient and supportive, and the chemistry between them had been undeniable from the very beginning.

Phoebe had felt that if they could face the horror of losing a baby together, then they could face anything. How wrong she had been.

TWENTY-TWO

It was late when Phoebe emerged from Ida's room, after having spent some time with her, listening to her mother-in-law reminisce about the early years of her marriage to George, before they had Mark. They were stories which Phoebe had not previously heard, and she was content to sit and listen, offering words of comfort when needed. She had encouraged Mark to go and have a lie down before she went to sit with his mum, so Phoebe tiptoed up the stairs now, careful not to wake him. When she poked her head around the door, though, he was sitting up awake and looking at his phone.

"How's she doing? Thank you so much for keeping her company."

"She's as well as can be expected. I think she might sleep for a bit now. I should, ah, be going," Phoebe said it with all the conviction she could muster, which was barely any.

Mark checked the time on his phone, "It's after ten, are you sure you want to head back this late?"

"I have my new position starting tomorrow."

They looked at each other silently. Neither wanting to be the first to suggest she stay the night, but it was clearly what they both hoped for. The air in the room was charged with tension and with what went unspoken between them.

Eventually, taking in his red-rimmed eyes and considering Mark had only picked at his food, Phoebe's concern for him won out. It was purely altruistic on her part, it had nothing to do with the fact that she couldn't bear the thought of parting from him, of course.

"I could email them and say I'll be there on Tuesday instead. I'm sure they'll understand when I explain it's a family bereavement."

"Really? Thank you, Phoebs, thank you, I'd appreciate that."

"You're welcome, honey. Let's get the house locked up and try to get some sleep, shall we?" Phoebe tried to focus on the practicalities, rather than the knowledge that they were about to share the bed together again.

Phoebe lay on her side, facing away from Mark, with him spooned up against her back. She could feel his even breathing on her neck and his arm slung around her waist effectively pinning her against him. They had cuddled briefly when they got into bed, then exhaustion claimed them, and both had snuggled down on their separate sides. At some point in their sleep, they must have assumed this position, a favourite when they were together. Phoebe didn't mind – in fact, she was enjoying being so close to Mark again. It was easy, in the dark and in this familiar place, for her to pretend that he did not live five thousand miles away, and that their lives were not now very separate.

Mark's breathing changed and she could tell he too had woken up. Phoebe froze, pretending to be asleep, but it was too late.

"Phoebs?" he whispered against her ear, his beard tickling her skin gently.

"Mhm?"

No reply came. Instead, his thumb began tracing a pattern against her stomach, under her top which had ridden up. Phoebe snuggled back, closer against him, feeling his arousal pressing against her. She knew fine well the signals she was giving off by doing so, and at this point didn't care. They needed each other. They were married still. What was one last goodbye?

She turned in Mark's arms to face him, their noses almost touching. In the moonlight that shone through the crack in the curtains, Phoebe could just about make out Mark's features. His expression was a mixture of question and desire and Phoebe answered his unspoken enquiry by leaning in and taking his mouth in a searing kiss. This was not a quick peck of comfort, of reassurance or for old-times' sake. This was the full measure of her love and passion, six-months' worth, all rolled into one.

The kindling was lit and the fire exploded into energy and light. Neither shied away from it, neither paused to question the consequences, or whether, once re-lit, it could be extinguished again. They let their bodies say what their words had not, and their only guide was their enduring love

TWENTY-THREE

Monday morning found Phoebe and Mark naked in each other's arms. They awoke late and lay snuggled up for a moment before either of them spoke. Neither knew what to say. Both had an ache in their heart, knowing that they needed to part again, and they put off the moment for as long as possible. Mark was grieving and his mum needed him there, after which he would fly back to his new life in California. Phoebe had her research, and hopefully a new life in Hawaii if and when her funding materialised. They were no longer a single unit, as much as it had felt like they were in the dark hours of the morning.

"I'll let you use the bathroom first, I know you need to get going," Mark's tone was distant and dismissive.

Phoebe understood why. He was protecting his heart, and she knew she'd need to do the same. That didn't mean it didn't hurt though. That his words didn't cut her, ripping open the wound that she had lived with these past six months. Phoebe slipped into the en suite without a word, careful not to let him see the tears trickling down her face.

She caught sight of herself in the bathroom mirror, her long curls a tangled mess, her lips red and swollen from his kisses. Phoebe turned away at the picture of herself, of the well-loved woman who was now a weeping mess again, and stood for longer than usual under the shower, letting the strong jet of water wash away the reminders of the night with her husband. When she emerged from the bathroom she would be ready to make a fresh start – another one – and to put their reunion behind her.

Mark had already gone downstairs when Phoebe slipped back into the bedroom. She dressed and dried her hair quickly, before packing her things into her bag and rushing downstairs. Ida was up, and fussing over Mark in the kitchen, so Phoebe did not linger. She couldn't. If she even stayed one more minute than she absolutely had to, her resolve would fail. Especially as she knew how much he was hurting, how much he needed her comfort at this time.

You could cut the tension with a knife, as Ida offered her breakfast and Phoebe politely refused. Mark didn't take his eyes off her the whole time. Dark and brooding, Phoebe didn't want to try to interpret their meaning. Instead she hugged Ida, promised she would keep in touch and would certainly come for the funeral, said goodbye to Mark, pecked him quickly on the cheek and turned to leave.

"Phoebe?" his voiced halted her in her tracks.

Following her into the hallway, Mark stood staring at her. Phoebe was frozen to the spot, pretty certain that anything they said now would just make things worse. She was taking the coward's way out – avoiding discussion of what had happened between them – and she knew it. But Phoebe couldn't face the alternative. Mark, however, couldn't seem to let her go without addressing it.

"Thank you. For everything," it was a pointed remark, with a huge sub-text, as Ida was listening from the kitchen.

"It was my pleasure," Phoebe whispered, willing her eyes not to fill up again until she got to her car.

He leaned in and kissed her softly on the forehead, "I love you," his breathy words hit her skin, and pierced her heart. Phoebe stepped back from the force of his declaration, knowing that Mark had not said it out of habit this time.

"I love you too," she had to respond with the truth. To leave without saying it would have been cruel. Once the words were out of her mouth, however, Phoebe turned and fled the house, not stopping until she was in her car and had the engine in gear. Then she allowed herself one small look.

Mark stood framed in the doorway, his mother's roses arching over him. He held up a hand in farewell, and Phoebe did the same, before driving off and out of the cul-de-sac. She had to park up in the next street though, as she couldn't see to drive safely through her tears. She would see Mark again before he went back to the States, of course, but that would be at the funeral, when he would quite rightly be focused on other things. Phoebe would not go to the wake, just pay her respects to Ida after the service and then leave. No chance for uncomfortable encounters with her spouse. Why did that leave her feeling so hollow? So sick to her stomach? Phoebe brought her emotions under control and drove off, determined that she needed to start focusing on the future. A future that did not include Mark.

TWENTY-FOUR

Mel was at work when Phoebe arrived at their flat. She had argued with herself the whole drive back, part of her knowing she should have stayed with Mark, the other part needing to make a break now before she was sucked too far back in. The result was a churning stomach, a splitting headache, and a confusion that left her on the verge of tears the whole time.

Swilling back a glass of water with a couple of paracetamol, Phoebe noticed a post-it note on the counter-top next to the kettle. It was from Mel, saying how sorry she was to hear about Mark's dad, that there was chocolate cake in the fridge, that Jack had popped round twice looking for her, and that she wanted all the 'deets' about Phoebe and Mark when she got home from work. Phoebe couldn't face the chocolate cake, even though it was kind of Mel to leave her favourite comfort food, nor did she have any headspace for Jack right now. One man in her life at a time seemed to be too much at the moment, let alone two! All Phoebe wanted to do was to curl up in her bed and shut everything out for a few hours. The supervisor at the lab had replied to her email saying that she should take a few days, and start on Thursday instead, for which Phoebe was very grateful. Her life felt as if it were spiralling downward again, as it had in the days after Mark had left.

By a stroke of very bad luck, the letter explaining that her funding request was on hold had come just two days after Mark had left to begin his new life. The irony had not been lost on Phoebe, who had spent the week in a daze of tears and disbelief. She had been so sure that this was her year to make her dream a reality. So sure in fact, that she had gambled her marriage on it. And lost.

It was four in the afternoon, when Phoebe was awoken by the doorbell. She must have cried herself to sleep, she guessed, as the last time she'd looked at the clock it was just past noon. Dragging herself down the hallway, Phoebe was shocked to see Carlos. That is to say, at first all she saw was a large bunch of roses, and then Carlos poked his head around the enormous bouquet.

"Oh, hello!" Phoebe wasn't sure what to say, her mind was still foggy.

"Hello, Phoebe, I was hoping to see Melanie, if she is home?"

"I'm sorry, Carlos, she's at work."

"Oh yes, silly me, the work," Carlos looked genuinely despondent when he realised the time, "I finished early and I did not think, I was just so eager to see her…"

"Would you like to bring the flowers inside?" Phoebe had no desire to communicate with anyone, yet she couldn't very well close the door in his face either – it would squash the roses!

"Thank you, Phoebe," Carlos deposited the bouquet carefully on the kitchen table before turning to face Phoebe, who hovered in the doorway to the kitchen. He looked her up and down, not in a lascivious way this time, rather with an expression of concern. Phoebe knew what a state she must look – the old joggers and t-shirt she had hastily thrown on, her hair scraped back in a messy ponytail and her swollen, red-rimmed eyes.

"Are you okay?" It was said softly, and Phoebe knew that even those simple words were likely to trigger her waterworks again.

"Thank you, I'm…" she replied, unable to speak further through the lump in her throat.

"Do you need anything?" Carlos moved to the glass-fronted kitchen cabinet where he could see a row of mugs. He opened it, took one and filled it with tap water before handing it to her.

"Here, drink this senhora!"

"Thank you," that did it, the tears were falling uncontrolled now, and Phoebe couldn't hold them back. Carlos stood, wringing his hands uncomfortably. "You don't need to stay if you need to get going," Phoebe whispered, trying not to sound dismissive after he had been so kind to her.

"No, I have the time," he pulled two chairs out from the kitchen table, and Phoebe accepted the seat, lowering herself gingerly, placing her mug shakily on the table and putting her head in her hands. To give him his due, Carlos didn't try to hold her, not even to rub her back, he simply sat down beside her and waited, patiently, for her to recover enough to speak.

"Thank you," it seemed to be all Phoebe was able to come up with, but it was enough. They sat in comfortable silence while she sipped at her water and tried to gather her thoughts. Thinking of Mark was too painful, so she focused on Carlos instead. Clearly, she had misjudged the man.

Eventually, seeing she was more composed, he spoke, "So, you like the albatross? And I don't mean the golf one this time!" he tried to buoy her with humour.

"Yes, since I was a girl!" It was a good choice of conversation. Safe, reassuring, and Phoebe went with it, "Did you know, they are the most efficient travellers of all the vertebrates on this planet? They soar hundreds of miles over the ocean each day, expending little energy as they don't need to flap their wings once they're aloft! They have a tendon in each shoulder which locks their wings fully-extended."

"No, I did not know that," Carlos replied. Phoebe studied him for any signs of mockery, but saw none. The sweet man seemed genuinely interested.

"Yes, and a Laysan – that's an island in the North Pacific, near Hawaii, I can't wait to visit though no-one lives there – sorry, a Laysan albatross named Wisdom who lives on Midway Island, is the oldest known wild bird in the world! She was tagged in 1956 and is almost certainly older than seventy!" Phoebe realised she was waffling now, eager to share the facts as they popped into her brain. Anything to take her mind off her husband.

"Wow! That is something! But is the albatross not considered bad luck?"

"Well, it was considered very bad luck in old maritime suspicion to kill an albatross," Phoebe dropped into morose silence once more, her desire to follow her ambition and career had certainly become the albatross around her own neck. At length, she continued, "In the poem of 'The Ancient Mariner', for example, when he kills the bird and the crew feel his doing so has brought them bad luck, they make the Captain wear the albatross around his neck to literally show his guilt and the bad omen he has brought them."

"And you? Has studying it brought you bad luck?" Carlos, keen to keep the conversation flowing and distract her, didn't realise the effect this question would have on Phoebe, whose sobbing renewed with vigour. "Oh, Senhora, my apologies," he looked to her helplessly, then to the clock on the kitchen wall which was now, thankfully, closer to five. He prayed Melanie would soon return.

"I'm sorry," Phoebe said through her tears.

"No need, I am glad to be here for you, but I worry I have distressed you more," Carlos tapped his finger on the table in agitation.

"No, thank you for staying. I didn't want to be alone with my thoughts today."

"I was going to take Mel out for a drink, to a place where the view over the town is fantastic! Perhaps, you shower and come out? I collect you both at seven?" His kind eyes looked hopeful.

Phoebe's immediate instinct was to refuse, until she thought about the long, lonely night laid out ahead of her.

"Thank you, Carlos, I would like that."

TWENTY-FIVE

Phoebe had tried to avoid telling Mel that she had slept with Mark, but the other woman had returned from work, taken one look at her friend's tear-stained face, and known there was more going on than losing her father-in-law. Over tea and chocolate cake, Phoebe had given the bare bones of the weekend's events, leaving Mel slack-jawed in shock.

"But, I thought it was over for good with you two?" she asked, incredulous, "You led me to believe something terrible had happened between you, from which there was no return and which caused him to not just leave Oxford, but to leave the continent! I thought he must have strayed…!"

"What? No! Mark would never... No, well, I may have downplayed my own part in proceedings," Phoebe admitted, "My reluctance to leave with Mark, because I was waiting for my big break."

"Do you think," Mel paused, trying to think of how she could word her question in a way that would not upset her best friend, "Do you think Phoebe, that perhaps grief from the miscarriage could have made you focus blindly on your albatrosses and your career. Something that was constant and tangible?"

Oof, that one hurt. Phoebe took a deep breath in, as if the words had been a physical blow to her abdomen. She simply nodded, it would be pointless to deny it. The truth, when stated so simply, hit hard. Of course, the thought had crossed her own mind several times, only to be summarily discarded and shoved back in its box. She couldn't let herself believe that she had shunned her husband, the new life he had fought for, for them both, and the chance to have a family in the future with him, because of blinding grief. When they had kept trying for a baby, and she didn't fall pregnant again in the months before Mark left, Phoebe had stubbornly taken that as a sign that her dogged focus on her career was the right path now. She had reached a crossroads, taken one road which had come to an extremely painful end, so now she would follow the other path with unwavering determination. Wouldn't she? Phoebe wasn't sure any more. Not after seeing Mark. Not after being in his arms again.

"I'm sorry," Mel whispered, seeing the pain on her friend's face, "I just mean that, maybe you weren't thinking straight for the six months before Mark left. That isn't a long time to try for a family again… Besides, things aren't set in stone, are they? Especially, now, not after the two of you have done the…"

"Mel!" Phoebe blushed and stood up to rearrange Carlos' beautiful flowers, which she'd had in a vase ready for Mel's return. Anything to keep her hands busy.

"Sorry, sorry! I just mean, well, there's still hope."

"No. There isn't any hope. It can't happen again!" Phoebe left the room to shower and change. Her head was a mess of tangled thoughts. Guilt and grief, plus a feeling that she had cursed herself to a life she was no longer sure she wanted. She knew Mel was trying to be kind, to help her sort through things, but Phoebe wasn't ready to face it all yet.

"So, this is the Duke's Course," Carlos opened the

wide door to the club house and ushered the two women in, "one of the courses owned by the Old Course Golf Resort," he did a strange little flourish with his arms to indicate that he liked this particular venue greatly, then directed them into the bar and restaurant area. Huge windows lined the far wall, and it wasn't the golf course below which caught Phoebe's attention, rather the view in the distance. The whole of St. Andrews laid out below them. Town, coastline, all of it. She stood frozen to the spot, admiring the beauty of the location.

"I hoped you would like it," Carlos said, coming to stand beside her, "sometimes it is good to see the bigger picture, no?"

"It really is," Phoebe replied, thinking that there was much more to this man than met the eye. Mel had clearly struck gold finally, and Phoebe intended to tell her friend so when they were alone again. For now, though, they followed Carlos to a table with a 'Reserved' sign, on the terrace, and Phoebe was glad the evening was warm enough to sit outside in her jacket. They had an uninterrupted view from here, and she was happy to let Carlos pull out her seat in a gentlemanly fashion and offer her a menu. As Mel and Carlos chatted easily about the food and the holes to be played here, Phoebe sat in her own thoughts, wondering what the bigger picture really was for her now.

TWENTY-SIX

When Phoebe awoke late the next morning she was glad that she didn't have to start her new job until later in the week. She had only had a couple of drinks with Carlos and Mel – who were clearly smitten with one another – before catching a taxi back to the apartment. Tossing and turning for hours, sleep would not come until finally, when the dawn light shone underneath her window blind, Phoebe had finally fallen into fitful dreams. She wasn't sure if time was going too slowly, or if life was spiralling too quickly out of her control. Either way, Phoebe felt unsettled and imbalanced. A problem she intended to solve with a brisk walk along the beach and an afternoon of writing her latest research paper. She even had the thought, not for the first time, to turn all of her knowledge and research on albatrosses into an actual book. Perhaps today was a good day to start? The first day of the rest of her life. So why did she feel so flat? Why did her mind insist on looking backwards and not forwards?

The weather was beautiful for a walk, as Phoebe locked the front door and headed down to West Sands. She had left her phone at home, determined to clear her head and make the most of the sun and beautiful location. She had only walked for about ten minutes along the sand when she had the uncomfortable sensation that she was being followed. No sooner had the thought crossed her mind, than Phoebe almost fell flat on her face with the force of being jumped on from behind. Her legs buckled and she shrieked in fright. Her only tangible thought was how stupid she had been to leave her mobile phone behind. No way to call for help now.

"Phoebe, Phoebe, I'm so sorry," the familiar voice, at first heard from a distance, became closer until Phoebe felt a hand under her elbow helping her to her feet. Not, however, before she was given a big, slobbery kiss on her cheek from a certain black Labrador.

"Eurgh," Phoebe wiped the wetness with her sleeve

and turned her annoyed gaze onto a very red Jack. She was not in the mood. Neither for the man nor his beast.

"I'm so sorry. Bad dog!" Jack shouted the rebuke, however Oscar was already only a speck in the distance, jumping in the waves. Jack looked mortified, reaching a hand out to touch Phoebe's cheek.

"No harm done!" Phoebe bit out, flinching away and moving out of reach. She made a show of brushing the sand from her knees before finally looking up at the repentant man opposite.

"How are you?" Jack spoke quickly to cover the awkward moment, "Your friend mentioned there'd been a bereavement in the family?"

"Oh? She did? Well yes, there was," Phoebe didn't want to share any more details, her own face flushing at the memories of the weekend that rose unbidden to mind. Those of Jack and their night together were unfortunately swiftly overrun by those from the hospital, bringing with them much more stinging pictures from the mental movie-reel of her own bereavement the previous year. Phoebe blinked rapidly to clear the tears from her eyes.

"I'm so sorry for your loss," Jack offered, falling into step beside Phoebe, who was marching along the edge of the tide now. She knew she was being rude, and that the lovely man deserved better, but she simply couldn't cope with conversation right now.

After a few minutes of silence, Jack spoke up, "Is it because of my OCD?"

"Pardon?" Phoebe was as lost by the reference as she was by the sudden shift in subject. Still entrenched in her own thoughts, she couldn't make sense of the question.

"The reason you're so off with me? Since you saw my house, saw me acting that way?"

"No, no, I had no idea..." Phoebe stopped and turned to face the man. Jack avoided her gaze, his own face pale and haunted now.

"Really? Well, it's certainly a turn-off for most women!" his voice was hard and bitter, and Phoebe realised she had hurt the man in a way she had never intended.

"Listen, Jack," she tried to find the words that would soothe without having to divulge too many of her own demons, "it was my father-in-law who passed away. I've seen my husband and, and... well, we're maybe not as separated as I thought. I'm so sorry if I led you on in any way. I didn't mean to."

"Oh. Oh, I see. So, you didn't just decide you couldn't cope with my illness?" The poor man was almost beside himself with nervous irritation now. Embarrassed and uncomfortable, he hopped from one foot to the other, alternately ramming his hands in his pockets and then taking them out again to study his fingernails.

"Jack, listen," Phoebe reached out a hand to touch the sleeve of his jacket, "listen, I'm sorry I didn't pay more attention. I thought your house was clean and tidy, that you liked order and minimalism, I didn't read any more into it than that. I've been pre-occupied. I'm not ready for a relationship right now." She knew that she couldn't make it any clearer, couldn't spell it out more for him.

Jack swallowed, then stood perfectly still "I had hoped that we might... I mean, I know it was only one date, but I felt a connection... Well, anyway, it's fine, really, I'm sorry I assumed. It's just every woman so far has run a mile as soon as I've let them in. That, that... that part of me repels people."

"Well, it doesn't repel me, if you need a friend to talk to anytime. Right now, the timing's not so good, but in the future I'll be there if you need a shoulder to cry on… or a woman's perspective."

"Thank you," Jack hovered awkwardly, before calling Oscar and raising one hand in goodbye to Phoebe. As he turned to walk away, Phoebe was reminded of another sorrowful man who she'd hurt, one who had also raised one hand in farewell. Apparently hurting people was what she did now, even when she didn't mean to.

TWENTY-SEVEN

Trudging back up Golf Place to the flat, well over an hour later, Phoebe felt nowhere near as refreshed and clear-headed as she'd hoped to be after her walk. There had been that awful interaction with Jack, but really her state of mind could hardly be considered his fault. Indeed, Phoebe thought morosely, the poor man had probably come off much worse for knowing her than she had from the brief time she'd spent with him. Likely he would avoid women for quite a while now. Another layer of guilt to add the walls she was creating around her heart. Walls that only one person seemed to be able to penetrate.

As if she had conjured him by the sheer process of bringing him to mind, Phoebe approached her new home to see a familiar figure sitting on the doorstep.

"Mark?"

"Hi."

"Hi?"

"Er, sorry to bother you, Phoebs, but I remembered you said you weren't starting work till Thursday."

"Mhm," she tried to hide her secret pleasure at seeing him again. Mark stood and Phoebe squeezed past him to open the door. Careful not to touch, though her body was aware of him even without the contact. She walked through to the kitchen, her senses reeling and her heart screaming at her to walk straight into his arms. Jack closed the door quietly and followed. Then they stood there, looking at each other, the air thick with the tension and chemistry between them.

Finally, Phoebe could bear it no longer. Mark looked worse than he had yesterday morning when she'd left him. Was that only yesterday? His short beard had become even more straggly, his face grey and sad. So sad. Phoebe was so touched by the sight of him that she moved closer, until they were standing toe-to-toe, and she looked up into his eyes. Mark lifted his hand slowly, watching her keenly for any sign that she might flinch away, signalling that his touch was unwelcome now. When he saw none, he cupped Phoebe's cheek in his palm, lowering his forehead to rest on hers.

"Phoebs, I'm sorry. I know you don't want to see me here, in your 'new start' place," he whispered.

"How did you find the address?" she wondered aloud, avoiding the issue.

"I tried to call you a few times to let you know I was coming. Then, I still had Mel's number from the miscar... from before... so I phoned her to get the details. Sorry."

"Shh, stop apologising. It's okay. I stupidly left my phone here when I went for my walk. How's your mum? You haven't left her alone?"

"No, Mrs. Grange from across the road stopped by and Father Michaels is expected to visit in an hour, so I thought I'd take the opportunity..." Mark paused, looking at her intensely, and Phoebe had the impression he was having an internal debate with himself. At length, he continued, "I need you, Phoebs."

It was so direct, so compelling, exposing his vulnerability to her, that Phoebe raised both her hands, cupping his face now as he still held her cheek, "I'm here, honey, I'm here for you."

Mark turned his face into one of her palms, and Phoebe felt the wetness of his tears against her skin. Closing the distance between their faces, she gently moved her hand to behind his neck, so that she had access to his lips, and brushed hers against them tasting the saltiness of his tears. So gentle, just the merest contact. Done without thought.

It was a tiny spark, but it ignited the fires in them both once again. There was no point fighting it, it was a force more powerful than them both. Besides, Phoebe had no desire to deny either of them the comfort they desperately needed. She pressed herself against him, and held him tightly around the waist, as she felt Mark's hands in her hair and on her neck and collarbone, his fingers tracing a path which left her trembling and brought goosebumps to her arms.

"Mark," she whispered, eventually pulling away slightly, "let's talk, I can make a pot of tea and we can sit on the sofa. You can talk to me about your dad, I know how much you must be missing him."

"Okay," his voice was gravelly and his face wet from tears and kisses, "but, after we've talked, can I… can I just hold you for a bit?"

The request hit Phoebe like another gut punch. She was getting quite a few of those lately. It wasn't that it was something difficult to agree to, or which she didn't need just as much as him, rather it was the hopefulness in Mark's tone, and the implication that the strong need was mutual, which moved Phoebe.

"Of course," she kissed him quickly on the lips before pulling away and out of reach so that things couldn't overflow again.

Sat on the sofa, with her arms around his shoulders, Phoebe leaned back against the armrest so that Mark could rest his head on her chest, just below her shoulder. She kissed the top of his head through his hair and rubbed her hands in slow motion. Slowly, she felt the tension leaving his body and he relaxed against her.

"So, how was yesterday?" she asked quietly.

"Pretty awful. As you'd expect. Visits from relatives, phone calls. Mum's up and down…" he trailed off, in thought again.

"I'm sorry I left so quickly after we got up," and she was.

"It's okay. I wasn't sure what to do for the best either. In the end, I thought putting some distance between us would be most sensible. Even though it hurt so much to push you away," he reached up and kissed her gently, before snuggling back down again.

"I know, me too. I can't tell you how many times I've wanted to drive straight back," she leant in and returned the kiss, this time lingering for longer.

"Really? I got the impression you were glad to get away?" Mark sat up then, to judge the truth in her answer by looking Phoebe straight in the eyes.

"Really. In fact, it was almost as hard as when you walked out with your cases and left me in the flat in Oxford," Phoebe whispered, "though I know I had no right to feel that way, after I'd told you so many times to go without me. I was just shocked when you did!"

Mark's teeth clenched and she saw the muscle in his jaw harden as he took on board what she'd said, "That was the worst … the second worst day of my life. The first was losing our baby. And there I was losing you too. It nearly killed me."

Phoebe didn't have the words to make up for either the hurt he'd suffered or the time they'd lost. Besides, nothing had really changed for their relationship in the past few days. They still had separate lives on different sides of the Atlantic. So, she stood up abruptly and moved to look out of the window, to the people passing by outside oblivious to her personal turmoil. Of course, Mark followed immediately, coming up behind her and lacing his arms around her waist.

As she let him pull her back against his hard body, Phoebe leant her head back on Mark's chest and wondered why she had let things become so difficult. Once upon a time, their love was enough. They had believed that they could face any obstacle together. Now, it felt like a tenuous link in a world which was pulling them apart. Or maybe she was the only thing insisting they go in different directions? Phoebe closed her eyes against the possibility.

TWENTY-EIGHT

Mark held Phoebe to him, as she turned in his arms and cuddled up into his chest. They stood there, each deep in their own thoughts. He was riddled with grief and regret. Grief for his dad, for his marriage and for losing the woman he loved. He couldn't seem to unravel any of the different strands, it was just one huge ball of pain inside him right now. The only time the weight of it seemed to lesson was when he was with his wife. He desperately wanted her to be his again. Not in a chauvinistic, possessive way, but in the way they'd vowed before God that they would be. Two halves of one whole. Yet, he knew that if he hadn't come back to Scotland, they likely wouldn't have seen each other for months, years even. Until the distance between them was too great to be surmountable. This was his only chance, but it would mean offering her a life in the States again, and Phoebe had made her views on that quite clear last Autumn.

It was too much. He should be grieving for his dad, and instead he was trying to save his marriage. Or was he? What was even the point?

Phoebe felt the sudden coolness against her body as Mark retreated away from her. He stood a few feet away, his head in his hands, his back hunched. *I've done that to him*, she thought to herself, walking up behind Mark and rubbing a circle on his back. When Mark turned to look at her, the devastation on his face was clear to see. In that instant, Phoebe had the overriding desire to make him feel better. She couldn't sort the conundrum in her head, but she could offer him a brief comfort. They had done it once, what harm would one more time do? Phoebe knew the answer to that, knew that every time they re-consummated their relationship, it made it all the harder to part. Nevertheless, for the moment she was ruled by her heart and so she took Mark's hand, registering the surprise in his eyes as she led him to her bedroom.

It felt so right, all of it, and now Phoebe lay naked in Mark's arms for the second time in as many days, snuggled up in the afterglow of their love.

"Phoebs?"

"Mhm?" she turned her face up towards him.

"I can't keep doing this."

"Oh!" Phoebe sat up suddenly, his words cutting her.

"I mean," he was quick to expand, pulling her back into his embrace, "I want to be doing this with you. Of course I do! It's the parting I can't stand. When I lost you, I lost myself. It's not something I can do again and again!"

"Mark, I don't know how…"

"Shush! Just listen for once! Your dreams are my dreams. I'm only alive when I'm with you. One of the things that attracted me to you in the first place was how driven you are. I've just been existing over there without you, Phoebe!" his voice rose as his words became an impassioned plea, "Please, Phoebs, let's work this out!"

"We live thousands of miles apart, Mark!" her uncertain tone betrayed the conviction she'd wanted to convey.

"But you aren't settled here! You just got here, in fact, and you're studying seals of all things! You could join me there anytime you chose!"

"Well," Phoebe tried to rein in her growing indignation, "perhaps you could move here?"

"But I earn more there, I have career prospects and I'm closer to the North Pacific, that hallowed land you seek!" he struggled to keep the sarcasm from his voice.

Just like that, they had fallen back into the same argument, the same routine. They each knew their part so well, were so well rehearsed, that they almost didn't hear what they were saying anymore.

"Besides," Mark added, "I thought we agreed, we wanted to start a family. How can we do that living so far apart?"

Phoebe tried not to show how much those words stung, "That was BEFORE, Mark! Before the miscarriage!" The word which she so avoided. Which had become taboo between them. There, she'd said it!

Mark had no stinging retort, in fact his face crumpled, and Phoebe felt his emotions mirrored in herself. They had made the decision to take that path, walked it hand in hand, and then faced a devastation that had rent them apart. They had grieved together at the time, but subconsciously, Phoebe had chartered a new route for herself. One which her husband could either join or leave as he wished.

It was that which had led them here. To another impasse.

Mark rose from the bed quickly, grabbing his trousers from the floor and shoving his hand angrily into the pocket.

"Here, you might as well have this now!" he tossed her a parcel over his shoulder as he pulled the material over his legs.

Phoebe noted the Christmas wrapping paper and said nothing. Sitting up, covering herself with the sheet, she opened the package slowly and carefully. Inside, in a jeweller's box, was a solid silver bangle.

Mark was facing her now, bare to the waist still.

"What is this, Mark?" she whispered, though it was obvious that it was her Christmas gift. Remembering the day in December she had spent getting drunk alone, sobbing whilst she watched romantic movies,

Phoebe dragged herself back to the present.

"It's something I had ordered for you before we split. Then, I was going to post it for Christmas and… never got round to it. You might as well have it – it's engraved for only you."

"Oh," Phoebe turned the bracelet to see the inscription carved inside the band. It said simply 'Wisdom.' The name of her favourite albatross. Tears sprang to Phoebe's eyes.

"I bought it to show you, I know how important it is for you – your dreams are my dreams, Phoebs… Were my dreams, anyhow."

He stalked from the room, grabbing his top and shoes as he left. The tears rolled down Phoebe's face and she knew in her heart that this time she had really lost him.

TWENTY-NINE

The realisation hit Phoebe too late. Too late she understood that the root of the problem was her. Not Mark, not the tardiness over the grant proposal, not the beautiful area of Fife where she now lived. No one else was responsible for the failure of her marriage, for losing her husband not once, but twice!

When Mark had left, she had sat, stunned and devastated, twirling the silver bangle over and over between her fingers. He had not once said that she couldn't follow her dream. Indeed, he'd thought he was making it easier for her by applying for jobs in America. No, it was she who had seen it as an all or nothing issue. So black and white. She was a mother or she was a scientist. There was a baby then there was none. Phoebe's whole body had convulsed in sobs as she thought of all that she had lost over the past year. And now, when Mark was suffering another of the biggest losses of his life, she had encouraged him to focus on her and to grieve once more for their relationship rather than for the father he loved.

She had spent the next full day in bed, fobbing a worried Mel off with talk of a migraine, until Phoebe decided she had sunk into self-pity and self-recrimination long enough. She would begin her new job, make the best of it, move on and start afresh. Leaving Mark free from the baggage and burden she brought to his life. He deserved a fresh start even more than she did.

"Feeling better?" Mel's face was awash with concern when Phoebe eventually appeared in the kitchen on Wednesday evening. Phoebe could tell by her friend's expression that she clearly didn't look better. In fact, she was sure she must look a state, with her hair not having been brushed, her face still covered in dry tears.

"I'm well enough," was all she replied, walking into the hug which Mel offered.

"I'm seeing Carlos, but I could stay in tonight if you

prefer?"

"No, it's okay, I need to get my head in gear for work tomorrow. You go on out. How's it going? He seems nice."

"He is, and I think it's going well. Let's hope the Melanie jinx doesn't strike again!" Mel referred back to their time at university, when everyone she went out with turned out to be either two-timing her, or pre-occupied with drink, drugs or work.

"I have a feeling you've broken that bad luck once and for all," Phoebe tried to sound reassuring, but her voice was dull and flat. She accepted the mug of coffee which Mel offered and they both took a seat at the table.

"So," Mel ventured hesitantly, "I'm guessing this has to do with Mark?"

"It does. I mean, it did, but it's finished for good now. I think we just needed some kind of… closure."

"And did you get it?"

"Get what?"

"The closure?"

"I, well, we, um…" Phoebe had no answer. She twirled

the bangle absentmindedly. A permanent fixture on her wrist now.

"I see. You know, Phoeb, it's not too late to go back with him when he leaves after the funeral. If you think about it, it really was a stroke of luck that you moved up here. Otherwise you wouldn't have been close enough to go visit when Ida called you. You wouldn't have seen Mark again!"

"It is too late, Mel, it really is," Phoebe felt the tears choking her again, "I need to let him move on. I've been so selfish. I'm not so sure about the stroke of luck, but thank you, by the way, for offering me your spare room and letting me know about the job. I'm not sure if I ever said that. I've been so self-absorbed."

"Phoebe Ross," Mel turned and took both of her friend's hands in hers, "You lost a baby. Then you lost the chance to follow the studies you wanted…"

"That's not lost, just…on hold in the system!" Phoebe interrupted woefully.

"Okay, okay, so your research is on hold, but you lost your marriage, your home in Oxford. You've had a lot on your plate. You're perfectly entitled to have a wallow! Besides, I wasn't being totally altruistic – I needed a new lodger to help with the rent!" Mel winked as she finished, to soften her words.

"I don't know what I want any more, Mel, but I have to make the best of what I'm left with…I'm sorry, that wasn't meant to sound ungratef…"

"Shush! I know what you meant. Just know that I'm here for you!" Mel stood, rubbing Phoebe's shoulder lightly before leaving the room to dress for her date.

Phoebe sat cradling her mug in her hands, trying to find the energy to sort herself out for work tomorrow.

The doorbell rang as Phoebe was walking along the hallway to her room. Hearing the shower going, she reluctantly went to answer it, finding Carlos there.

"Good evening, Senhora," he smiled, a cautious expression which was far from the flirty gaze he had levelled at her when they first met, "how are you today? Mel said that you have been unwell?"

Feeling like he could see through her façade, as she muttered, "I'm fine," Phoebe shuffled awkwardly to the side to let the man in.

"You have had the bad news?" Carlos persevered, taking in the bedraggled woman before him.

"I, well, there was the bereavement, yes," Phoebe replied, referring to George, but then realising she could just as easily be talking about the grief of losing Mark again.

"A very difficult thing, grief," Carlos responded, sage as always.

"I think Mel may still be in the shower," Phoebe tried to change the subject.

"No worries, I can tell you about my clients today. Very funny, actually…"

Phoebe knew he was being polite, trying to allay her discomfort, and she was grateful as they headed into the kitchen together and he recounted the exploits of his day.

THIRTY

The first couple of days in her new job had been fine. Not great, but fine. Phoebe knew she wasn't giving it her full attention, which was neither fair to her new colleagues nor to herself, but she struggled to focus for any length of time. When her mind wasn't straying to Mark, and what he must be feeling, organising his dad's funeral, it was with the life in Oxford which she had left behind. On Saturday morning, when the wind was blowing strongly from the East, and the dark, overcast sky reflected her mood, Phoebe took a walk along the ancient stone pier, then back through the cathedral ruins. Deep in thought, she didn't see the man and dog until she was almost face to face with them, giving Phoebe no opportunity to walk in the other direction. Not that she had any reason to, she decided, since she and Jack had parted on friendly terms.

"Hello gentlemen," Phoebe greeted Jack, bending down to stroke a very excited Oscar behind the ear.

"Hi, Phoebe, how are you? I think we're the only ones silly enough to brave the elements today! Where's spring gone?" Jack spoke quickly, his nerves evident.

"I'm okay, thank you. I was just thinking about a hot chocolate," Phoebe fibbed. She hadn't thought any such thing, but she couldn't face going back to the empty flat as Mel and Carlos were on a jaunt to Edinburgh.

"Oh, really? Well, that's perfect. Shall we drop Oscar at home and go to the new tearoom on Market Street?"

Phoebe had no idea which tearoom he meant, but she was happy enough to follow along, "Sounds lovely."

When they reached Jack's home, Phoebe was shocked when he immediately invited her in. She clearly needed to work harder at disguising her thoughts, however, as Jack was quick to explain, "I'm working on inviting people back here more," he said, blushing, "especially those who I've told about my condition."

"Of course, that sounds a great idea," Phoebe offered as he led her into the pristine sitting room.

Oscar bounded into the kitchen where his water bowl and crate awaited, clearly ready for a nap. It made Phoebe wonder though, why a man with a mental illness such as OCD would choose to have a messy, fur-shedding animal. She wondered whether she should voice the question, when Jack anticipated her thoughts once again.

"My sister urged me to get him," he said ruefully, "And by urged, I mean she presented him to me as a birthday gift. A done deal. She knew I'd never abandon him once I'd held him, you see, I was very lonely…"

"I understand," Phoebe replied, "I'm sorry I didn't pick up on your condition. It's not like it's something I'd never heard of, an acquaintance in Inverness struggled with the same thing, I've just been very absorbed in my own problems.

"No, Phoebe, you'd barely met me. I was just being hyper-sensitive and paranoid thinking one visit to my home could turn you off so completely."

"Let's just say we were both caught up in our own misperceptions," Phoebe added, hoping to alleviate the blush from Jack's face. He really was a lovely, kind-hearted man, she thought, but not for her. He deserved someone whose heart was free and open. The thought that hers was very much closed to anyone but her husband, made Phoebe sad all over again. That boat had sailed and now she was stranded without even a paddle. Anyone who offered her a berth was likely to face the same rejection as Jack. She wondered how long that would be the case. Would she always feel she belonged to Mark?

"Jack, I feel I owe you an apology," she was making a habit of that this week, and so she should, Phoebe decided, "I probably gave off the impression that I was free to date again. And I was. Or rather, I thought I was. Turns out I've still got a lot… to work through." Phoebe bowed her head, willing the tears not to fall. It seemed like that was all she could rely on lately – her over-stimulated emotional response.

"None needed," Jack shood his head and smiled gently, "we went on one date, it wasn't like you'd made any commitment. And don't worry about not picking up on my OCD, it's different for everyone so what you've seen in the past me not be how it presents for me. There's no 'one size fits all!'"

"I know, and thank you, I feel like you're letting me off

the hook."

"Not at all. Now, I have hot chocolate, I have cream and marshmallows – a guilty evening pleasure of mine! – how about we have our drinks here?" he looked hopeful, and Phoebe couldn't have refused even if she wanted to. She needed all the friends she could get right now.

They sat in comfortable silence for a while, each enjoying their drink, Oscar lying happily in front of the fire which Jack had lit in the sitting room.

"No music lessons today?" Phoebe ventured.

"No, I had my two usuals first thing, then I had a new student starting at eleven, an older lady, but she cancelled at the last minute."

"Oh, I'm sorry, I hope she rebooks," Phoebe smiled over her mug.

"Me too! Anyway, tell me about your job, it's up past East Sands isn't it?"

"In the Gatty Marine Lab, yes. Thanks, it went okay. It's always hard to settle into somewhere new."

"It certainly is," Jack looked thoughtful, as if he

understood exactly what she meant, "is it what you wanted?"

His question could be interpreted so many ways in her current situation, that for a moment Phoebe just sat pondering it. Eventually, she replied, "No, to be honest Jack, no it isn't what I hope for or wanted in any way."

Before she realised she was saying it, Phoebe recounted the whole of the past year. Her devastation at the pregnancy loss, her new-found blinkered focus on her career, Mark leaving, and then the half a year of loss and loneliness which had ended with her here, in St. Andrews.

Jack listened patiently, only interrupting to request the occasional clarification. When Phoebe was finished, he had come to sit next to her and had a hesitant arm around her shoulder. Phoebe realised that she was crying now – fat, silent tears of exhaustion and defeat.

"So," Jack spoke when her tears had reduced to the occasional sniffle, "so, your husband is in Perth, grieving for his father. And you are here, grieving for him. Why don't you go to him, Phoebe? Believe me, there have been times when I haven't made the move, and I regret it now. You have so much more at stake than I did…"

"It wouldn't be fair, Jack, I just seem to keep hurting him."

Jack made a non-committal grunt and simply rubbed her back, leaving Phoebe wondering if there wasn't some sense in his words after all.

THIRTY-ONE

It was on Tuesday of that new week, when Phoebe received the text she had been dreading. The funeral details. There was no question but that she would attend. She owed it to the man she had seen as a father-figure, to his wife who now mourned him, and to their son whom Phoebe still loved. And love him she did. He was the last thing she thought about at night and the first image she saw in her mind every morning. The service was set for Friday at eleven, giving time for family members to come from further afield. Phoebe tamped down the nausea which seemed to be her constant companion this week, and bought a new black dress for the event, deciding that nothing in her wardrobe was quite sombre enough for the occasion.

Phoebe had politely refused Mel's kind offer to accompany her on the day, even just to drive Phoebe to Perth and wait in the car.

"Really, Phoeb, are you sure? You're looking quite peaky. You haven't been eating properly and I'd rather come with you. Dan at the lab won't mind."

Dan, Phoebe's new boss, had been very understanding of her need for Friday off, as well as for the many minor mistakes she seemed to have made since she'd started a week before. Phoebe grimaced. She wasn't usually someone who needed to be 'carried' at work.

"Really, Mel, thank you, I'll be fine. Service, then home. I won't hang around," they both knew what she meant by that, so Phoebe didn't bother to expand. Even talking seemed to exhaust her.

The church was made from dark stone, set in a graveyard on the outskirts of Perth, made to seem darker by the constant drizzle which drenched it. Phoebe was met at the door by Father Michaels, who escorted her to a seat on the front pew, assuring her that he'd been told she should sit with the family. Phoebe felt uncomfortable waiting there alone as the church filled up, wondering now if she'd been right to refuse Ida's offer to meet them at the house and follow behind the hearse. It couldn't be helped now. She must wait.

Before long, the cloying smell of incense had Phoebe's head reeling, mixed with the sound of the old organ and the quiet chatter of the mourners in the pews behind. She felt sick and faint, and was just about to leave through the side door for some fresh air when a change in the music indicated that the funeral procession had arrived. Phoebe stood along with the rest of the congregation and was relieved when Mark was finally standing next to her, Ida on his other side. He had helped his mother down the aisle with her arm though his, and sat her down at her reserved place, then turned to glance at Phoebe.

His own face was ashen and taut, but what he saw on his wife's features must have shocked him, as Mark immediately leaned over and whispered, "What's wrong, Phoebs?"

"I'm okay," she whispered back, desperate not to cause a scene as the service began.

When Mark reached out to take her hand during the prayers, his shoulders shaking from the force of trying to hold back his tears and be strong for his mother, Phoebe accepted his touch gladly. In return, she offered what little strength she had, what little reassurance she could give, by moving her thumb over his palm to let him know she was there for him. As the family stood to walk into the graveyard behind the coffin, with Mark at its front corner, Phoebe linked arms with Ida and helped the woman out and over the slippery grass, to where a freshly-dug grave waited. It was the sight of that which broke the poor woman, and Phoebe held Ida as she battled the emotions which tore through her. His sorrowful task complete, Mark came to join the two women as the words were spoken, the prayers said, and the coffin lowered into the ground, 'ashes to ashes, and dust to dust.' It was as his mother threw a single white rose onto the varnished wood of his dad's last resting place, that Mark broke down completely. Turning into Phoebe, she drew him into her embrace, holding him close and trying to absorb some of his pain. If she could have taken it all for him, Phoebe knew that she would have. As it was, all she could offer was a wet shoulder and words which she hoped might bring some comfort.

The service finished, Mark asked if he could join Phoebe in her car to go to the small, local hotel where he'd hired a function room for the wake. He didn't want his mum to have the work of everyone coming to the house, and had always found the church hall quite antiquated and grim. It reminded him none-too-fondly of lonely birthday parties as a child. So a hotel it was. There was only one funeral car now, for Ida, Uncle Alan and George's other brother, William, to ride in, so Phoebe had no choice but to agree. It was not that she didn't want to be as amenable as possible, rather that this made her plan of a quick exit impossible, and forced her to spend some time at the wake. As they made their way along the gravel paths of the cemetery, back to the main road where Phoebe had parked, Mark directed her to a small bench under a group of trees. The wooden seat turned out to be too wet to be of use, so they hovered awkwardly beside it.

"You sure you're okay to drive, Phoebs?" he asked, his red-rimmed eyes studying her closely, "I could drive."

"Sure, thanks," Phoebe knew that would set alarm bells ringing for her husband, as it was the first time she had ever given up the wheel to him, but she felt so sick and dizzy still that she decided it was not safe for her to drive again until she'd had a bite to eat.

"Okay, honey, let's go," Mark's worry lines were clearly visible as he offered Phoebe his hand and they walked with fingers linked the rest of the way, each deep in their own thoughts.

THIRTY-TWO

The wake started as a quiet affair, but as George's golfing buddies began to reminisce, and drinks began to flow, the small, basement room with no windows became suffocating to Phoebe. She had sat politely beside Mark and Ida, nodding when necessary, fielding questions from Mark's extended family about when she would be joining Mark in America, and when they were planning to give Ida a little grandchild to distract her. Eventually, when it all became too much, she made her excuses and intended to slip away.

Mark had been watching her like a hawk the whole time, however, so Phoebe knew such a plan was futile. The moment she had hugged Ida and shook hands with the two uncles, Mark was by her side, following her up the stairs to the main foyer of the hotel.

"Phoebe!" His voice was plaintive, and Phoebe couldn't help but turn around to look at him.

"Mhm?"

"Phoebs, let's pop into the hotel coffee shop for a quick drink."

"I've had enough tea to sink a ship, Mark!"

"Okay, well, a soft drink then, whatever!" He guided her by the elbow into the small coffee shop off the main entrance area. Where Phoebe would normally be indignant at being told what to do, she was now just resigned. Exhausted, she let him lead her.

They bought two cans of coke for an exorbitant amount and sat at a small table in the window. The view was more grey buildings and a few trees, yet both seemed transfixed by it.

"I'm flying back tomorrow, Phoebs," it was Mark who broke the silence first, though his words did nothing to ease the tension. He reached his hand out across the table, and Phoebe extended hers to join with it. She wasn't sure what he wanted her to say to that.

"I'll miss you," she whispered, thinking of all the things she should have said the first time he left and didn't, "I want you to be happy, Mark."

"I'll only be happy if you come with me, Phoebe!" He raked his hands through his close-cropped hair. His beard had been trimmed short for the funeral and it gave him a more severe look than she was used to.

"Mark, I can't…"

"Well, I don't mean tomorrow, obviously, but soon, once you've tied up everything in St. Andrews?" he looked so hopeful. Phoebe knew this was the last time he would ask. She didn't even know anymore what was holding her back.

"I'm not sure, Mark, I don't want to leave you hanging. You deserve a fresh start."

"And I want that start to be with you, Phoebs!" he attracted the stares of an older couple on the table next to theirs when his voice rose in pitch and volume.

Phoebe simply sat and stared at him, willing herself not to cry again. Her head was pounding, almost as much as her heart. When the silence had drawn out for at least a minute, he shoved his chair back roughly, making it scrape along the floor.

"I guess that's your answer then!" he rose and moved swiftly from the table, leaving Phoebe feeling as if she was in shock. *We can't leave things like this. Not a third time!* Phoebe jumped up, grabbed her bag and ran after him.

"Mark!" he was already at the top of the small staircase when she caught up with him, ready to head back down to the gathering.

When he swung on his heels to face her, Phoebe took a step back. Mark's face was a picture of pain, and she felt ill at the knowledge that she had made him feel like that. Unwanted. Unloved. Rejected again.

"Yes?"

"Mark, I… I… I'll always love you!"

"And I love you, Phoebe," he said, though his voice was harsh and his anger and frustration evident, as Mark turned away and this time descended the stairs without looking back.

THIRTY-THREE

Phoebe could barely recall how she drove back to St. Andrews that day, only that she had to stop half way to throw up by the side of the road. When she finally got back and peeled off her clothes, she stood under the shower until her skin went wrinkly, trying to blot everything out. Mel must've gone straight out after work with the lab group for the usual Friday drinks, and Phoebe was glad of the peace in the flat to try to gather her thoughts. Except she couldn't. She felt too exhausted, too completely drained and so ended up falling into a disturbed sleep, slumped on the couch.

It was dark when Mel gently woke Phoebe. The moonlight shining through the curtains which were yet to be drawn. Phoebe accepted her friend's arm to help her into her bedroom, her head pounding and her legs weak. Of one thing she was certain, things could not go on like this.

Phoebe knew in her gut why she felt so unwell, why her whole life felt like it was falling apart before her eyes – she should have accepted his offer. Should have jumped at the chance to get back together with Mark. Goodness, the man had been patient enough these past two weeks. But now he was gone, back to America, back to his new life where he surely wouldn't be single for long. Mel threw herself into her work as best she could that next week, eager to try to move past the pain.

Out on a boat the following Friday morning just after dawn, a week to the day after she had last seen Mark, Phoebe was struggling to focus on her data collection and seal sightings. Indeed, she felt sicker than she had even these last few days.

"No sea legs, eh?" the skipper asked as she emptied what little contents she had in her stomach over the side of the boat.

"I thought you were used to this kind of research?" Tom, a colleague, asked, his tone condescending and sceptical.

Phoebe wanted to defend herself, argue that she was normally much better than this, but she found she had little energy. Staggering into the lab after the trip, Mel took one look at her and excused them both for an early lunch.

"So," Mel began when they were both sitting down. Mel had a baked potato with cheese and coleslaw and a cappuccino, but Phoebe could face only a cup of sweet tea, "so, tell me, when did you last have your period, Phoeb?"

"What?"

"Your period, is it late?"

"Well, yes, actually, but what has that got to do with anything?"

Mel simply looked at her compassionately as the realisation dawned on Phoebe that perhaps this was more than just a broken heart.

"I can't be," Mel whispered, "We tried the whole time after the miscarriage, right up until Mark left, and nothing!"

"But that was only six months wasn't it? You know it

can take much longer than that. And have you started taking your pill again since?"

"No, I wasn't in a relationship so I didn't think… Oh, no, Mel," Phoebe, to her embarrassment, began crying. Huge salty tears, which flowed rapidly down her face and landed on the table between them.

"Hush, it's not so bad is it?" Mel reassured, "besides, you might not be, it's probably just me reading into things!" she tried to backtrack slightly, but the seed had been sown.

"No, I have to go, Mel, thanks."

"Where? I don't think you should be by yourse…" But Phoebe had already rushed off, and the tinkle of the bell on the doorway of the café signalled her departure.

THIRTY-FOUR

Phoebe rushed blindly along North Street, past the University chapel, St. Salvator's, and down towards the flat. She fumbled in her bag for her phone, scrolling through her recent contacts.

"Hello?"

"Hello, Ida, it's Phoebe."

"Phoebe, lass, how are ye?"

"I'm okay, thanks Ida, how are you?" Phoebe tried to rush through the pleasantries but didn't want to be impolite or give cause for alarm.

"Aye, I've been a bit on the quiet side, lass, you know,

without George an' all."

"I'm so sorry, Ida. I'll come across to visit you soon, I promise. Tell me, do you happen to have Mark's number in California, or his address even?"

"Why lass?"

"Well, I want to contact him," Phoebe was trying hard not to give in to either exasperation or more tears.

"Aye, but he isn't in America."

"He's not?" her befuddled brain couldn't quite follow, "Is he on a field trip?" Mark often went to visit other telescopes or help with their installation or update.

"No, dear he's here. Well, he's not here."

"He is? But he's not?"

"Exactly. He was here, but he's gone out for some milk."

"Milk?" All Phoebe could do was parrot the woman's words back to her now. The implication of those simple sentences was huge.

"Aye, he stayed to keep me company, got special permission from the department head!"

"Okay, okay, thank you Ida....oh, Ida?"

"Yes, dear?"

"How long will he be with you?"

"I'm not sure lass, this weekend for certain."

Phoebe thanked her mother-in-law and hung up. She took a sharp left and hurried up Greyfriar's Garden back onto Market Street where she rushed into the supermarket and bought a double pack of pregnancy tests.

Back at the flat at last, Phoebe was on tenterhooks in the kitchen, two tests laid out on the table in front of her, her phone on a countdown for three minutes. The doorbell rang, and Phoebe cursed under her breath. She had a mind to ignore it, expect the caller was insistent.

"If this is Carlos with more flowers…" she muttered, rushing along the hallway and throwing the door open. It wasn't Carlos, though, nor Jack. It was, in fact, the only man who should be there to share this moment with her. The only man who mattered.

"Mark!"

"Hi Phoebs. I know we said that was it, and I know

you think I'm in the States…" he began waffling, as Phoebe stood looking at him, her mouth agape.

"Could you wait in the sitting room for a moment, Mark?"

"Well, yes, but Phoebe, I need to speak to you. I know you think everything's been said, but…"

"One minute… I've, I've left the hob on!" Phoebe rushed from the room, back along the hallway to the kitchen. Snatching up the tests, she peered at them, her stomach doing a little leap then falling with a thud inside her abdomen. She couldn't think straight, so she ran. Out of the still-open front door, into the drizzle without a coat. She needed air, she needed to quell her panic. She needed the only place that brought her calm.

THIRTY-FIVE

It had started to drizzle again and Phoebe had rushed out without a coat. She couldn't have cared less. She ran as fast as she could, down to West Sands and onto the beach. She assumed Mark would follow her, but she refused to look back. Gulping in lungful's of the salty air, Phoebe let the rain wash away her fear and allowed herself to feel the joy of the new life that was growing inside her. Suddenly, everything else fell away for a moment.

"Wait, stop!"

Phoebe came to a halt, the waves crashing beside her, the light drizzle beginning to drench her from above.

Mark, out of breath, his face a picture of worry, took a light hold of her arm to stop her running off again.

"What is it, Phoebe? Tell me!"

"Honestly?"

"Yes, yes of course, only the truth between us now!"

"I'm scared."

"Scared? Of me?" he recoiled, the horror in his face clear to see.

"No! Of course not."

"Okay," the relief was clear, "Of him, the other bloke. Was he angry when you told him you'd… been with me?"

"What? Jack? No, no, he wouldn't hurt a fly! We're friends, nothing more. Have never been anything more!"

Mark looked at her beseechingly, waiting patiently for Phoebe to continue. When she stood silently shivering, he moved in closer, running his hands up and down her arms in rhythmic reassurance, vowing to himself that he would hurt whoever had made her feel this way.

"We've been through some scary times together, Phoebs. Let me help you now." She had moved closer, imperceptibly, until now Phoebe stood with her head nestled under his. Mark's arms moved to her shoulders, rubbing circles against her blouse which stuck to her back it was so wet. Her hair fell in wet, brown ringlets and Mark gently brushed them from her face.

Her arms came around him, and his drew her even closer, until they held each other in a fierce hug. Eventually, Phoebe pulled back, but Mark caught her hands as she distanced herself. He held both in his larger palms and his thumbs moved in slow circles.

Phoebe cleared her throat uncomfortably, "When your dad… passed. We, er, spent a lot of time together."

"Yes?" Mark wasn't sure where she was heading with this. Surely that wasn't something to be afraid of? Though, when he thought on it, their future scared him too. Where did they go from here? "Is it our future that scares you?"

"Yes, but it's more than that… we spent the night together…and then the afternoon!"

"Yes, and it was…"

"I know!" she cut him off before he could tell her what she already knew. That it had been wonderful. The time had come, she needed to say the words. "We didn't use protection, Mark!"

Phoebe watched as confusion clouded his eyes, and then they cleared in a demanding question.

"Phoebe, you need to spell this out for me!" his voice was raspy with emotion. His hands on hers were still now, and he held them tightly as if she might run.

"I'm pregnant, Mark! And I'm scared stiff!"

As the truth was revealed and the full impact dawned on him, Mark's face morphed into one of delight and awe.

"Really, Phoebs?" his smile was huge and Phoebe couldn't help but smile back

"Really. I've taken a test, two tests actually, to confirm it."

He pulled her to him, careful not to press against her stomach, as if suddenly she was more fragile, breakable even. He looked down into her eyes, then to her mouth. Phoebe felt the invisible force attaching her to him, somehow stronger now than ever, and lifted her mouth to his in response. His kiss, when it came, was slow and tender, reverent in its care. Phoebe could almost not bear it. She needed his passion, his reassurance, his declaration that he was here for the long haul, so she pressed her mouth to his urgently, her tongue diving into his mouth in demand.

Mark paused, apparently slightly shocked, but only for a second. Then he met her with the force she needed, the delightful friction, their mouths melding together until suddenly, abruptly, he pulled away again. Phoebe lurched at the sudden cold he'd left.

"You're shivering, Phoebs, God you're freezing, and here I am kissing you, when I should be getting you somewhere warm!" he rebuked himself.

Phoebe simply smiled back at him, drenched through now. A rainbow had formed overhead as the rain began to ease off, and Phoebe let her husband lead her back up the beach, his arm around her shoulders, pulling her into him. And she knew. She knew without a shadow of a doubt, that they were home again.

A Stroke of Luck

Epilogue

A Stroke of Luck

EPILOGUE

It had been a month since Phoebe had left and, true to her word, she had kept in contact with Jack. On their last video call, she had excitedly shown him the apartment which she was now sharing with Mark in California, and the room which would become the nursery. She was having extra checks to monitor her pregnancy and the baby's growth, and her face had glowed with happiness. As luck would have it, her grant proposal had finally been approved, and she was planning a few research trips to Hawaii with Mark, where he would work on telescopes and she would spend a short while on Laysan island. From this research, she was planning to finally write the book about albatrosses that had been on her mind for years now.

Jack couldn't have been happier for them both, though he had to admit to feeling slightly sad too. Not from jealousy, rather from the feeling that it would never happen for him. He would not get his chance at love again. As he was about to take Oscar on yet another walk, the dog seemingly having boundless energy which was good for distracting Jack's thoughts, the doorbell rang. Answering it, to see a friendly smile, on a sweet face, Jack was suddenly struck mute. He needn't have worried, the lady was bubbly enough for both of them.

"Hello! I'm here for my first lesson!"

"First lesson?"

"Yes, on the piano! It's Hope. Hope Guthrie, we arranged via email?"

"Oh, yes, that was for the sixth of last month! I thought you had changed your mind!"

"I am so sorry. I am forever doing this. Ditsy, that's me!" she looked genuinely dejected.

"Not to worry, I am free now, as it happens…"

Follow Jack's story in the next book in the 'Found in Fife' series –

A Note of Hope

A Stroke of Luck

ABOUT THE AUTHOR

Rachel Hutchins lives in northeast England with her husband and three children. She works as a freelance proofreader and editor at ITP Proofreading and loves writing romance books. Her favourite place is walking along the local coastline.

As well as her contemporary stories under this name, Rachel also writes sweet historical romance under the pen name Anne Hutchins.

You can connect with Rachel and sign up to her newsletter via her website at www.authorrachelhutchins.com

Alternatively, she has social media pages on,

Facebook: www.facebook.com/rahutchinsauthor

Instagram: www.instagram.com/ra_hutchins_author

Twitter: www.twitter.com/hutchinsauthor

A Stroke of Luck

OTHER BOOKS BY R. A. HUTCHINS

"Counting down to Christmas"

Rachel has published a collection of twelve contemporary romance stories, all set around Christmas, and with the common theme of a holiday happily-ever-after. Filled with humour and emotion, they are sure to bring a sparkle to your day!

"The Angel and the Wolf"

What do a beautiful recluse, a well-trained husky, and a middle-aged biker have in common?
Find out in this poignant story of love and hope!

When Isaac meets the Angel and her Wolf, he's unsure whether he's in Hell or Heaven.
Worse still, he can't remember taking that final step.
They say that calm follows the storm, but will that be the case for Isaac?

Fate has led him to her door,
Will she have the courage to let him in?

Both books can be found on Amazon worldwide in e-book and paperback formats, as well as free to read on Kindle Unlimited.

A Stroke of Luck

HISTORICAL ROMANCE
BY ANNE HUTCHINS

"Finding Love on Cobble Wynd"

A small coastal town in North Yorkshire is the setting
for these three romantic stories, all set in 1910.
As love blossoms for the residents of Lillymouth,
figures from their past, mystery and danger all play a
part in their story.
Will the course of true love run smooth, or is it not all
plain sailing for these three ordinary couples?

Lose yourself in these sweet tales of loves lost and
found:

The Little Library on Cobble Wynd

Considered firmly on the shelf, Bea comes to the Lilly
Valley looking for a fresh start. She finds more
companionship than she ever hoped for in Aaron and
his young daughter, but is heartbreak hiding on the
horizon?

A Bouquet of Blessings on Cobble Wynd

When florist Eve discovers that her blossoming attraction for the local vicar may be mutual, she is shocked when his attentions run cold. Could danger be lurking in the shadows?

Love is the Best Medicine on Cobble Wynd

An unexpected visitor turns Doctor William Allen's world upside down and sets his pulse racing in this tale of unwanted betrothal.

A standalone novel, with happily-ever-afters guaranteed, these are the first of many adventures on Cobble Wynd!

"A Lesson In Love on Cobble Wynd"

In 1911, fiercely independent school teacher Florence Cartwright finds herself taking up lodgings in the home of widower and local constable, Robert Hartigan.

Whilst her host remains in an oblivious stupor, Florence does her best to help his three children with their own problems, putting herself in danger in the process.

When higher powers force the couple to form a relationship much closer than either of them would wish, will they be able to overcome their own frustrations and resentments, and move on to something more fulfilling for them both?

Whilst this second book in the Cobble Wynd series does feature some familiar characters from the first book, this story can certainly be read as a standalone novel.

Both books are available on Amazon worldwide in e-book and paperback formats, as well as free to read on Kindle Unlimited.

A Stroke of Luck

Printed in Great Britain
by Amazon